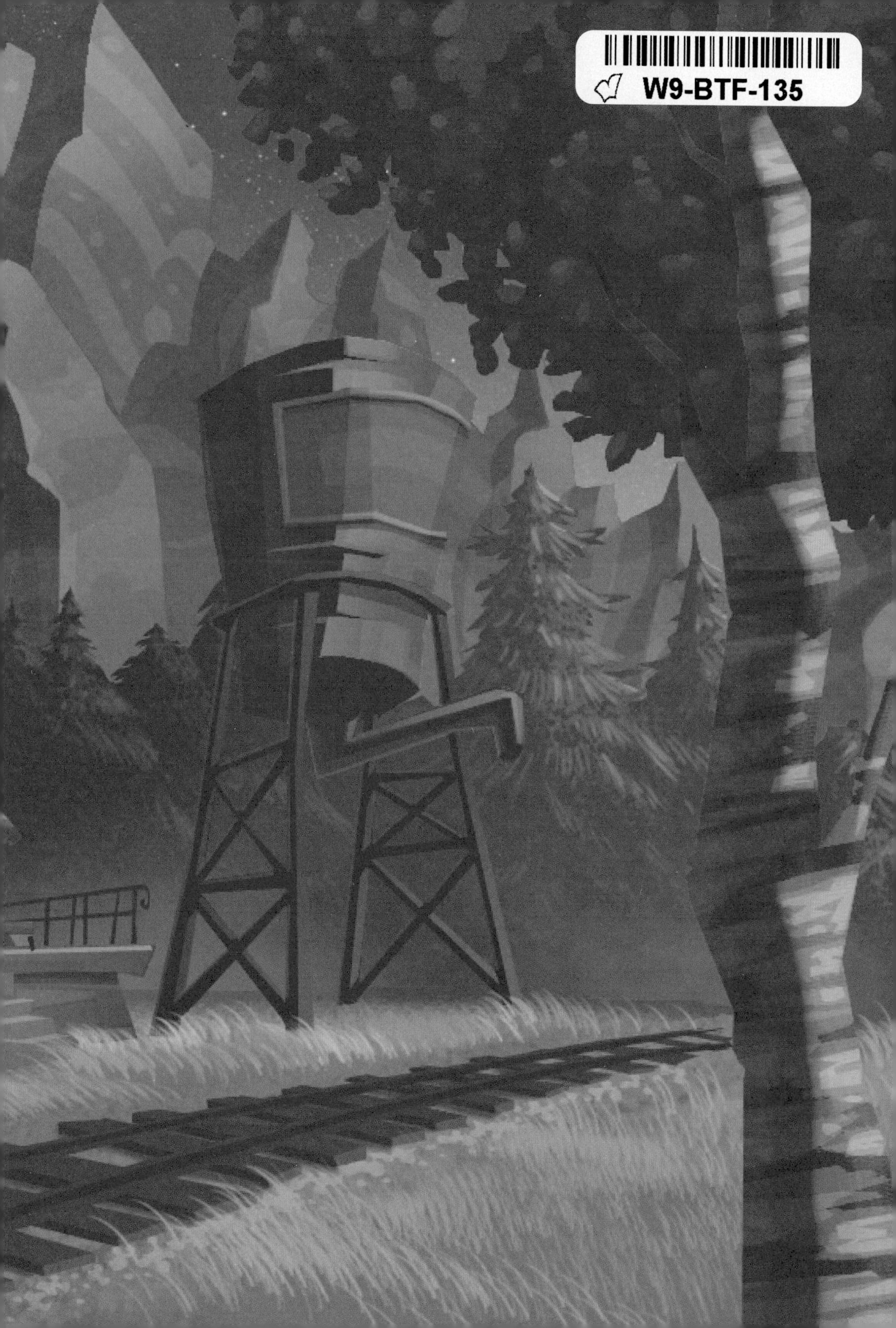

Geronimo Stilton™ Reporter

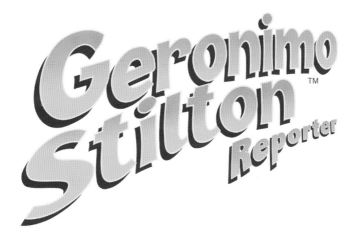

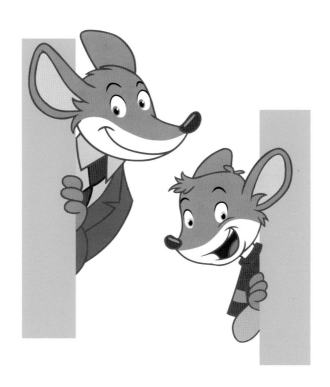

PAPERCUTZ™

Geronimo Stilton

GRAPHIC NOVELS AVAILABLE FROM PAPERCUTZ

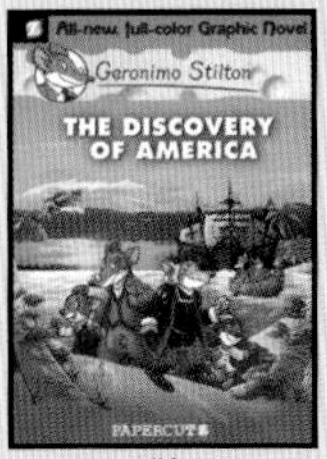
All-new, full-color Graphic Novel
Geronimo Stilton
THE DISCOVERY OF AMERICA
PAPERCUTZ

#1
"The Discovery of America"

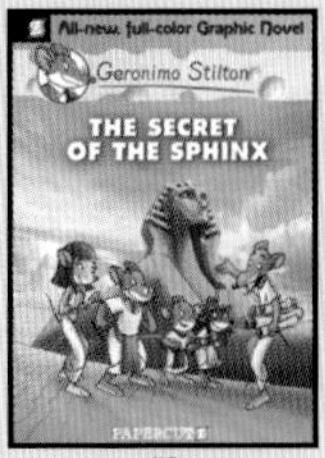
All-new, full-color Graphic Novel
Geronimo Stilton
THE SECRET OF THE SPHINX

#2
"The Secret of the Sphinx"

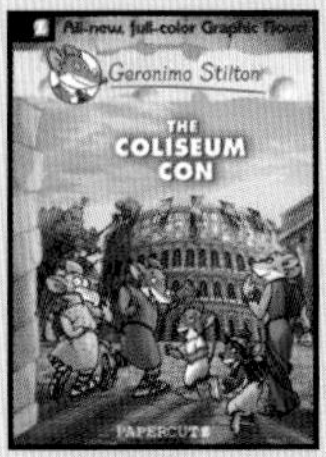
All-new, full-color Graphic Novel
Geronimo Stilton
THE COLISEUM CON

#3
"The Coliseum Con"

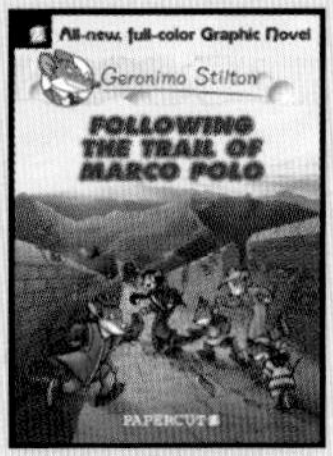
All-new, full-color Graphic Novel
Geronimo Stilton
FOLLOWING THE TRAIL OF MARCO POLO

#4
"Following the Trail of Marco Polo"

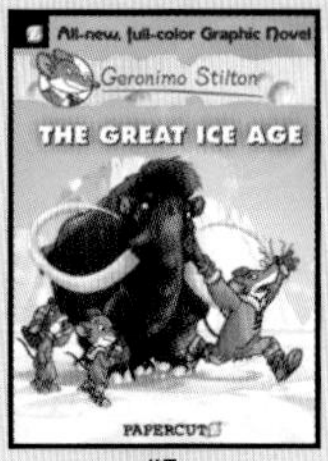
All-new, full-color Graphic Novel
Geronimo Stilton
THE GREAT ICE AGE

#5
"The Great Ice Age"

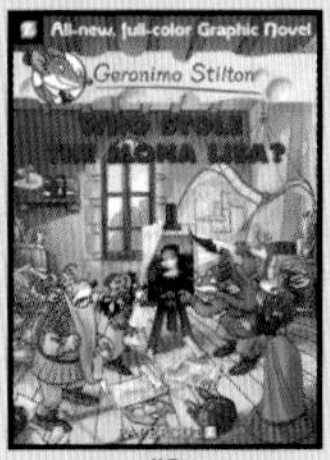
All-new, full-color Graphic Novel
Geronimo Stilton

#6
"Who Stole The Mona Lisa?"

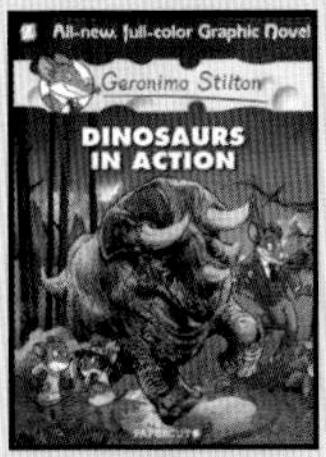
All-new, full-color Graphic Novel
Geronimo Stilton
DINOSAURS IN ACTION

#7
"Dinosaurs in Action"

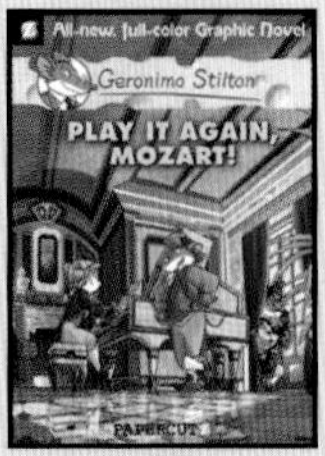
All-new, full-color Graphic Novel
Geronimo Stilton
PLAY IT AGAIN, MOZART!

#8
"Play It Again, Mozart!"

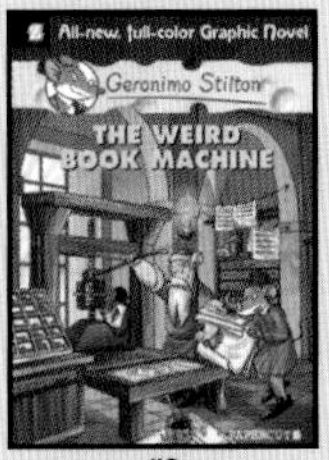
All-new, full-color Graphic Novel
Geronimo Stilton
THE WEIRD BOOK MACHINE

#9
"The Weird Book Machine"

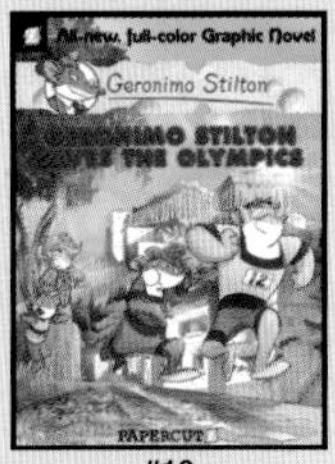
All-new, full-color Graphic Novel
Geronimo Stilton

#10
"Geronimo Stilton Saves the Olympics"

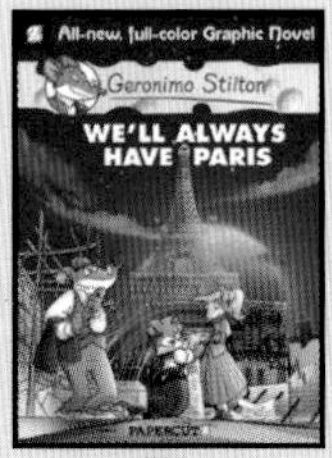
All-new, full-color Graphic Novel
Geronimo Stilton
WE'LL ALWAYS HAVE PARIS

#11
"We'll Always Have Paris"

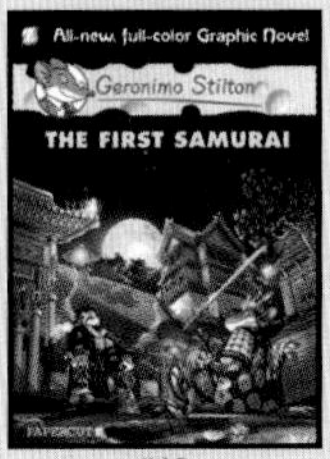
All-new, full-color Graphic Novel
Geronimo Stilton
THE FIRST SAMURAI

#12
"The First Samurai"

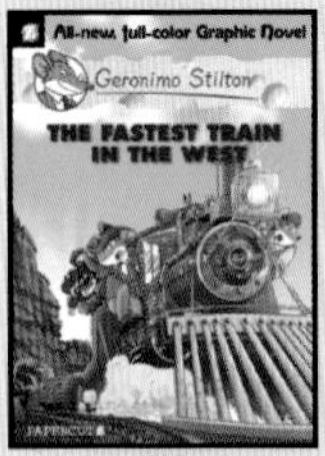
All-new, full-color Graphic Novel
Geronimo Stilton
THE FASTEST TRAIN IN THE WEST

#13
"The Fastest Train in the West"

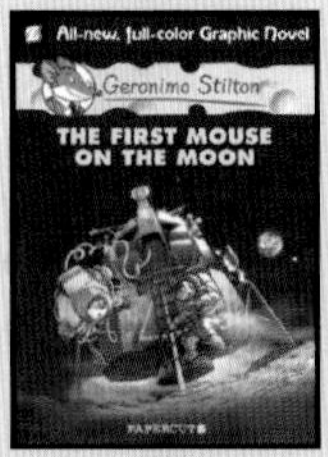
All-new, full-color Graphic Novel
Geronimo Stilton
THE FIRST MOUSE ON THE MOON

#14
"The First Mouse on the Moon"

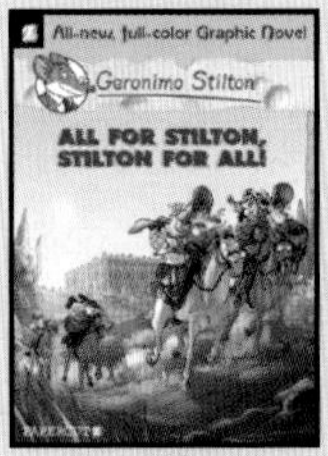
All-new, full-color Graphic Novel
Geronimo Stilton
ALL FOR STILTON, STILTON FOR ALL!

#15
"All for Stilton, Stilton for All!"

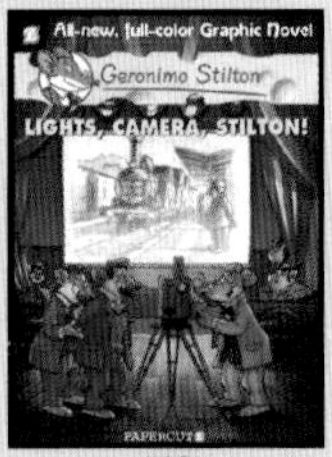
All-new, full-color Graphic Novel
Geronimo Stilton
LIGHTS, CAMERA, STILTON!

#16
"Lights, Camera, Stilton!"

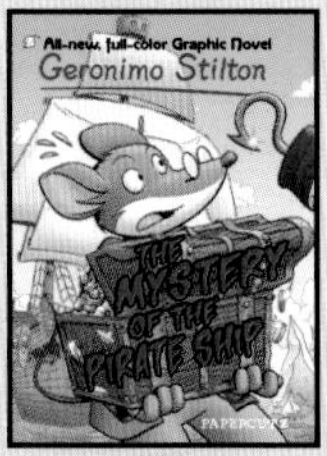
All-new, full-color Graphic Novel
Geronimo Stilton

#17
"The Mystery of the Pirate Ship"

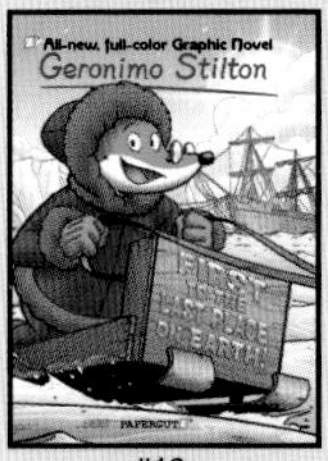
All-new, full-color Graphic Novel
Geronimo Stilton

#18
"First to the Last Place on Earth"

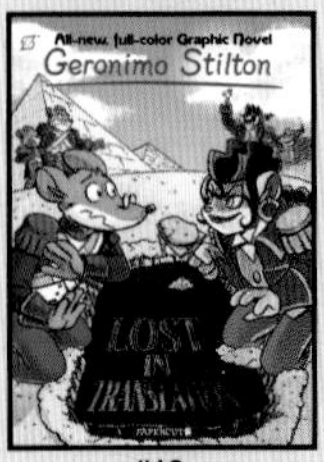
All-new, full-color Graphic Novel
Geronimo Stilton

#19
"Lost in Translation"

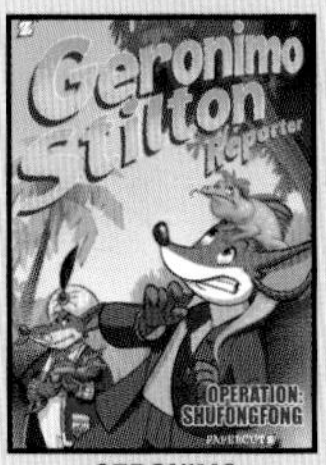
Geronimo Stilton
Reporter
OPERATION: SHUFONGFONG

GERONIMO STILTON REPORTER #1
"Operation ShuFongfong"

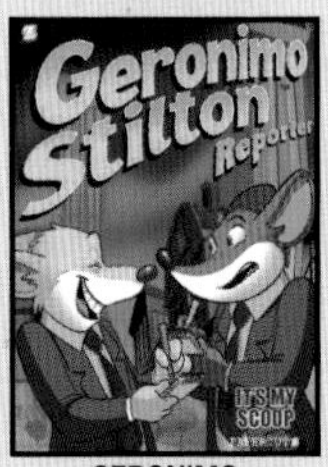
Geronimo Stilton
Reporter
IT'S MY SCOOP

GERONIMO STILTON REPORTER #2
"It's My Scoop"

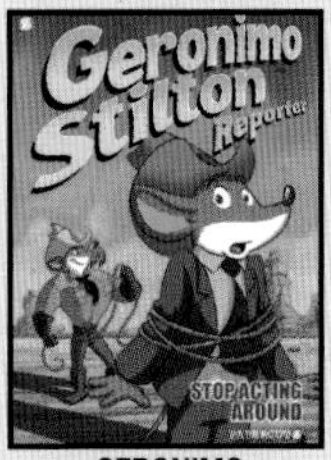
Geronimo Stilton
Reporter
STOP ACTING AROUND

GERONIMO STILTON REPORTER #3
"Stop Acting Around"

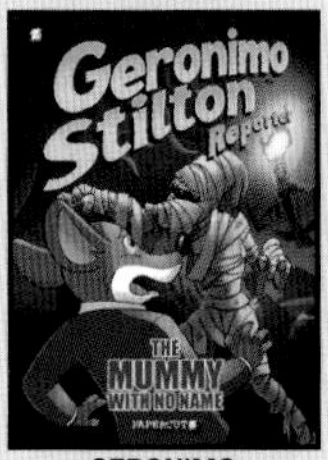
Geronimo Stilton
Reporter
THE MUMMY WITH NO NAME

GERONIMO STILTON REPORTER #4
"The Mummy with No Name"

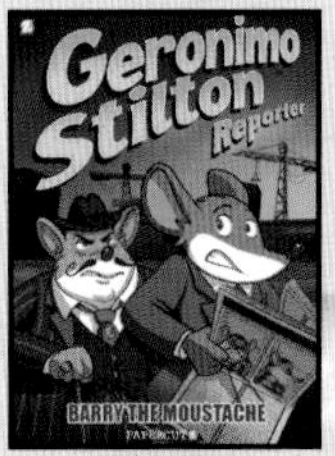
Geronimo Stilton
Reporter
BARRY THE MOUSTACHE

GERONIMO STILTON REPORTER #5
"Barry the Moustache"

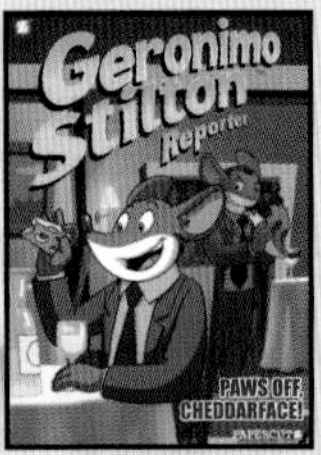
Geronimo Stilton
Reporter
PAWS OFF, CHEDDARFACE!

GERONIMO STILTON REPORTER #6
"Paws Off, Cheddarface!"

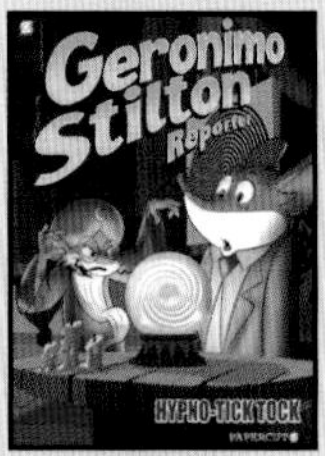
Geronimo Stilton
Reporter
HYPNO-TICK TOCK

GERONIMO STILTON REPORTER #8
"Hypno-Tick Tock"

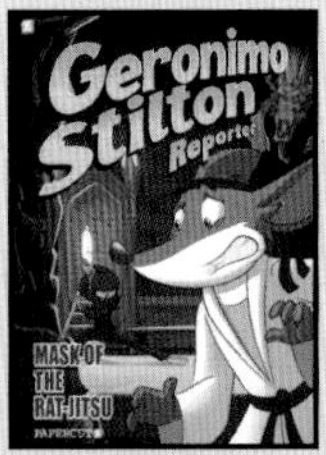
Geronimo Stilton
Reporter
MASK OF THE RAT-JITSU

GERONIMO STILTON REPORTER #9
"Mask of the Rat-Jitsu"

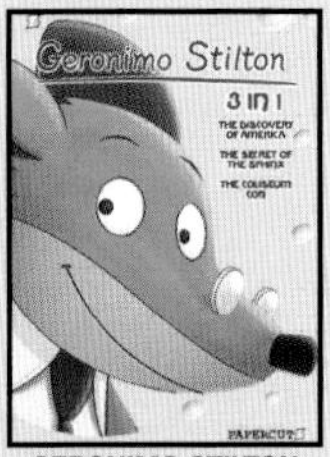
Geronimo Stilton
3 in 1

GERONIMO STILTON 3 in 1 #1

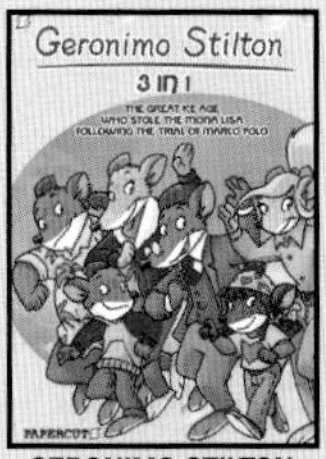
Geronimo Stilton
3 in 1

GERONIMO STILTON 3 in 1 #2

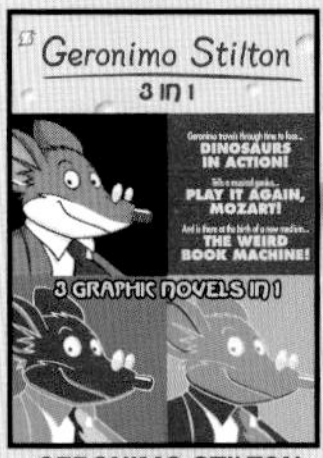
Geronimo Stilton
3 in 1
DINOSAURS IN ACTION!
PLAY IT AGAIN, MOZART!
THE WEIRD BOOK MACHINE!
3 GRAPHIC NOVELS IN 1

GERONIMO STILTON 3 in 1 #3

...ALSO AVAILABLE WHEREVER E-BOOKS ARE SOLD!

See more at papercutz.com

Geronimo Stilton Reporter ™

#11 MYSTERY ON THE RODENT EXPRESS
By Geronimo Stilton

PAPERCUT ™

NEW YORK

MYSTERY ON THE RODENT EXPRESS

Text by GERONIMO STILTON
Cover by ALESSANDRO MUSCILLO (artist) and CHRISTIAN ALIPRANDI (colorist)
Editorial supervision by ALESSANDRA BERELLO (Atlantyca S.p.A.)
Editing by ANITA DENTI (Atlantyca S.p.A.)
Script by DARIO SICCHIO
Art by ALESSANDRO MUSCILLO
Color by CHRISTIAN ALIPRANDI
Original Lettering by MARIA LETIZIA MIRABELLA

Special thanks to CARMEN CASTILLO

TM & © Atlantyca S.p.A. Animated Series © 2010 Atlantyca S.p.A.– All Rights Reserved
International Rights © Atlantyca S.p.A., Corso Magenta, 60/62 - 20123 Milano - Italia - foreignrights@atlantyca.it - www.atlantyca.com
© 2022 for this Work in English language by Papercutz, 160 Broadway, Suite 700, East Wing, New York, NY 10038
www.papercutz.com

Based on an original idea by ELISABETTA DAMI.
Based on episode 11 of the Geronimo Stilton animated series *"Intrigo sul Roditore Express,"* ("Mystery on the Rodent Express")
written by DIANE MOREL, storyboard by RICCARDO AUDISIO
Preview based on episode 11 of the Geronimo Stilton animated series *"Casa del Topo del Futuro,"* ("The Mouse House of the Future")
written by TOM MASON & DAN DANKO, storyboard by PIER DI GIÀ, LISA ARIOLI, & PATRIZIA NASI
www.geronimostilton.com

Stilton is the name of a famous English cheese. It is a registered trademark of the Stilton Cheese Makers' Association.
For more information go to www.stiltoncheese.com

JAYJAY JACKSON — Production
WILSON RAMOS JR. — Lettering
STEPHANIE BROOKS — Assistant Managing Editor
ZACHARY HARRIS – Editorial Intern
JIM SALICRUP
Editor-in-Chief

ISBN: 978-1-5458-0885-6

Printed in China
July 2022

Papercutz books may be purchased for business or promotional use.
For information on bulk purchases please contact
Macmillan Corporate and Premium Sales
Department at (800) 221-7945 x5442.

Distributed by Macmillan
First Papercutz Printing

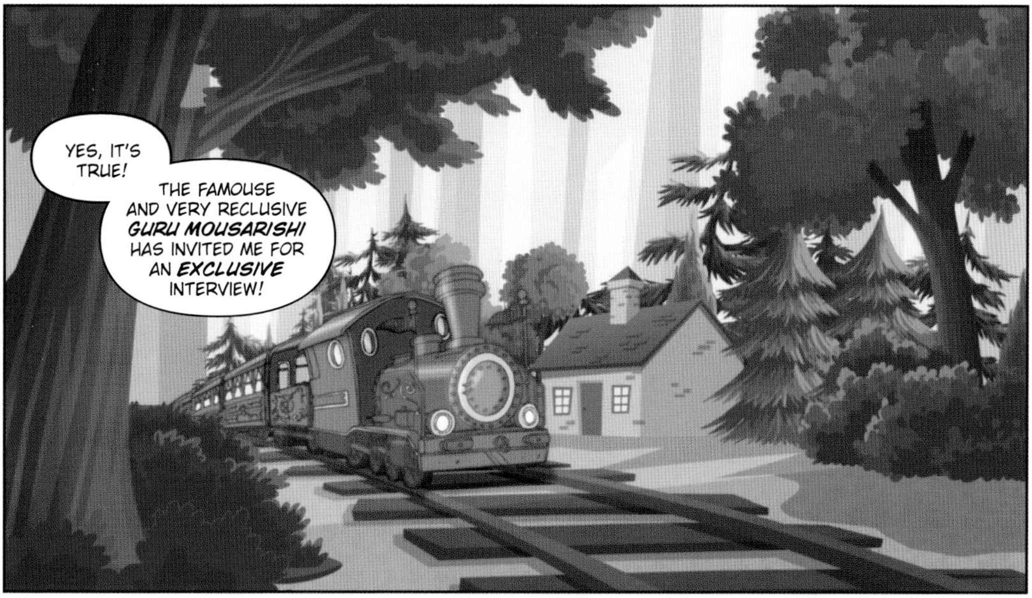
YES, IT'S TRUE!
THE FAMOUSE AND VERY RECLUSIVE ***GURU MOUSARISHI*** HAS INVITED ME FOR AN ***EXCLUSIVE*** INTERVIEW!

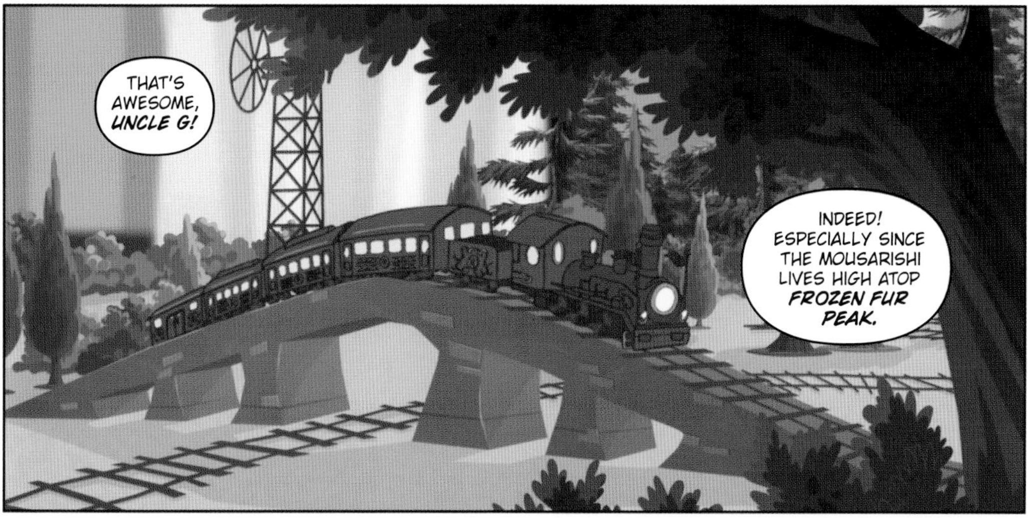
THAT'S AWESOME, ***UNCLE G!***
INDEED! ESPECIALLY SINCE THE MOUSARISHI LIVES HIGH ATOP ***FROZEN FUR PEAK.***

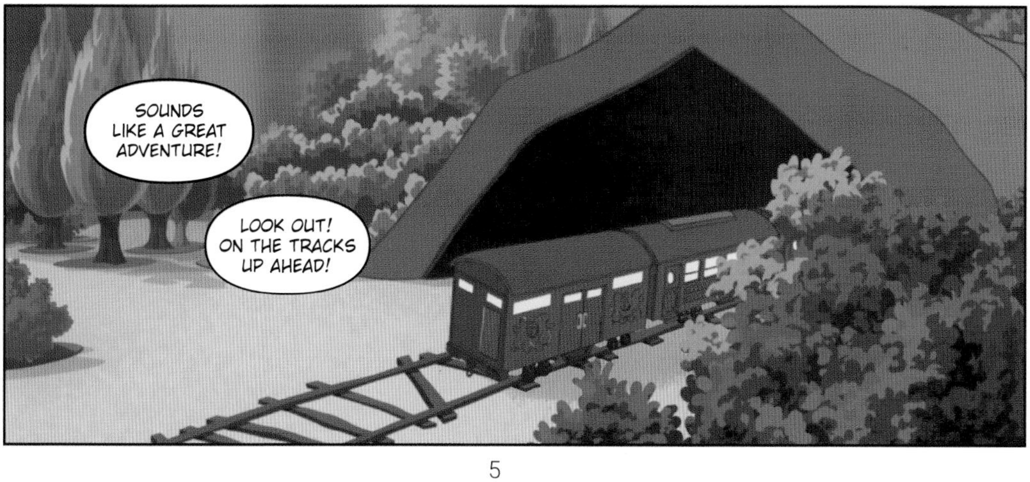
SOUNDS LIKE A GREAT ADVENTURE!
LOOK OUT! ON THE TRACKS UP AHEAD!

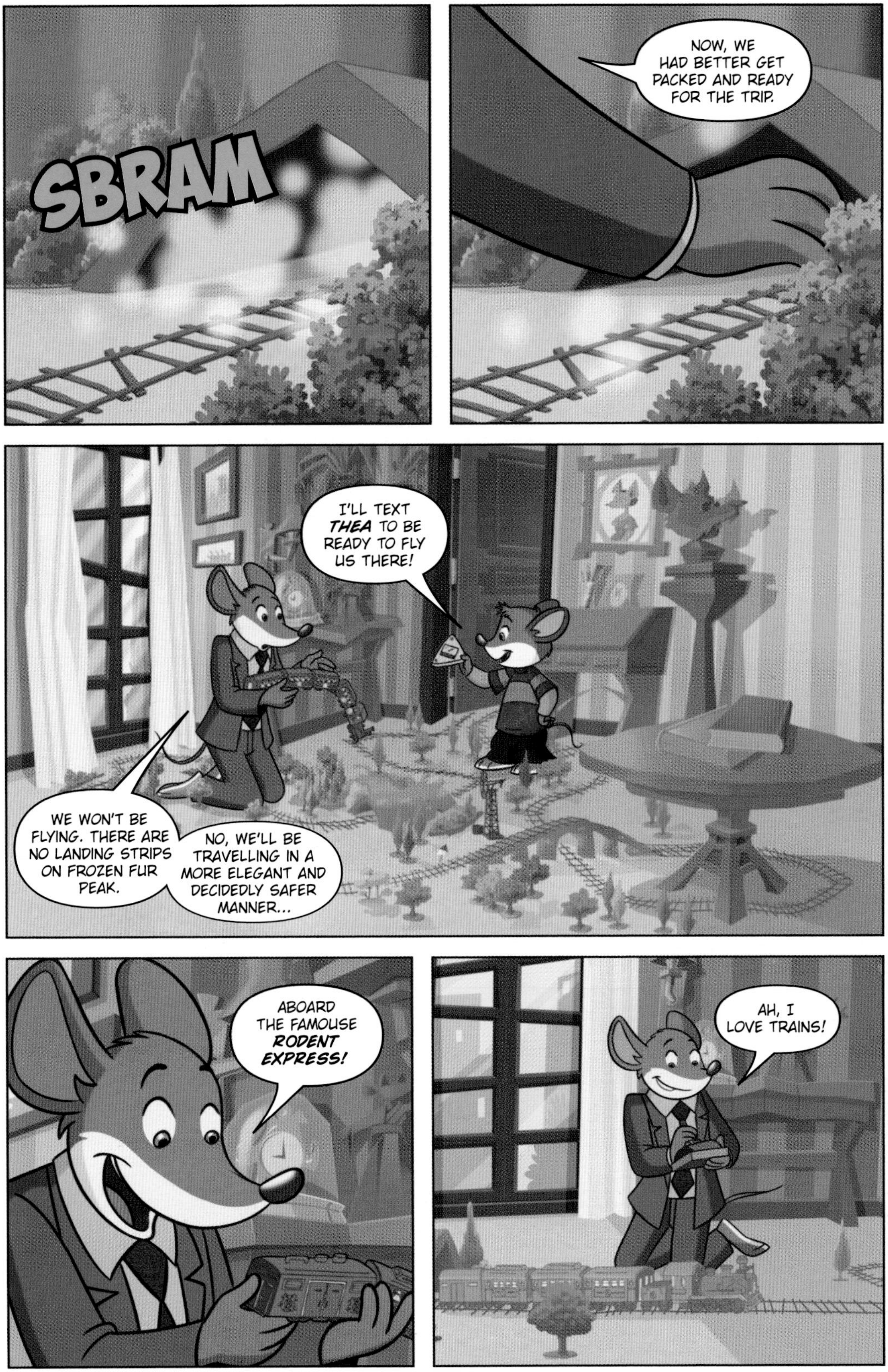
SBRAM
NOW, WE HAD BETTER GET PACKED AND READY FOR THE TRIP.
I'LL TEXT **THEA** TO BE READY TO FLY US THERE!
WE WON'T BE FLYING. THERE ARE NO LANDING STRIPS ON FROZEN FUR PEAK.
NO, WE'LL BE TRAVELLING IN A MORE ELEGANT AND DECIDEDLY SAFER MANNER...
ABOARD THE FAMOUSE **RODENT EXPRESS!**
AH, I LOVE TRAINS!

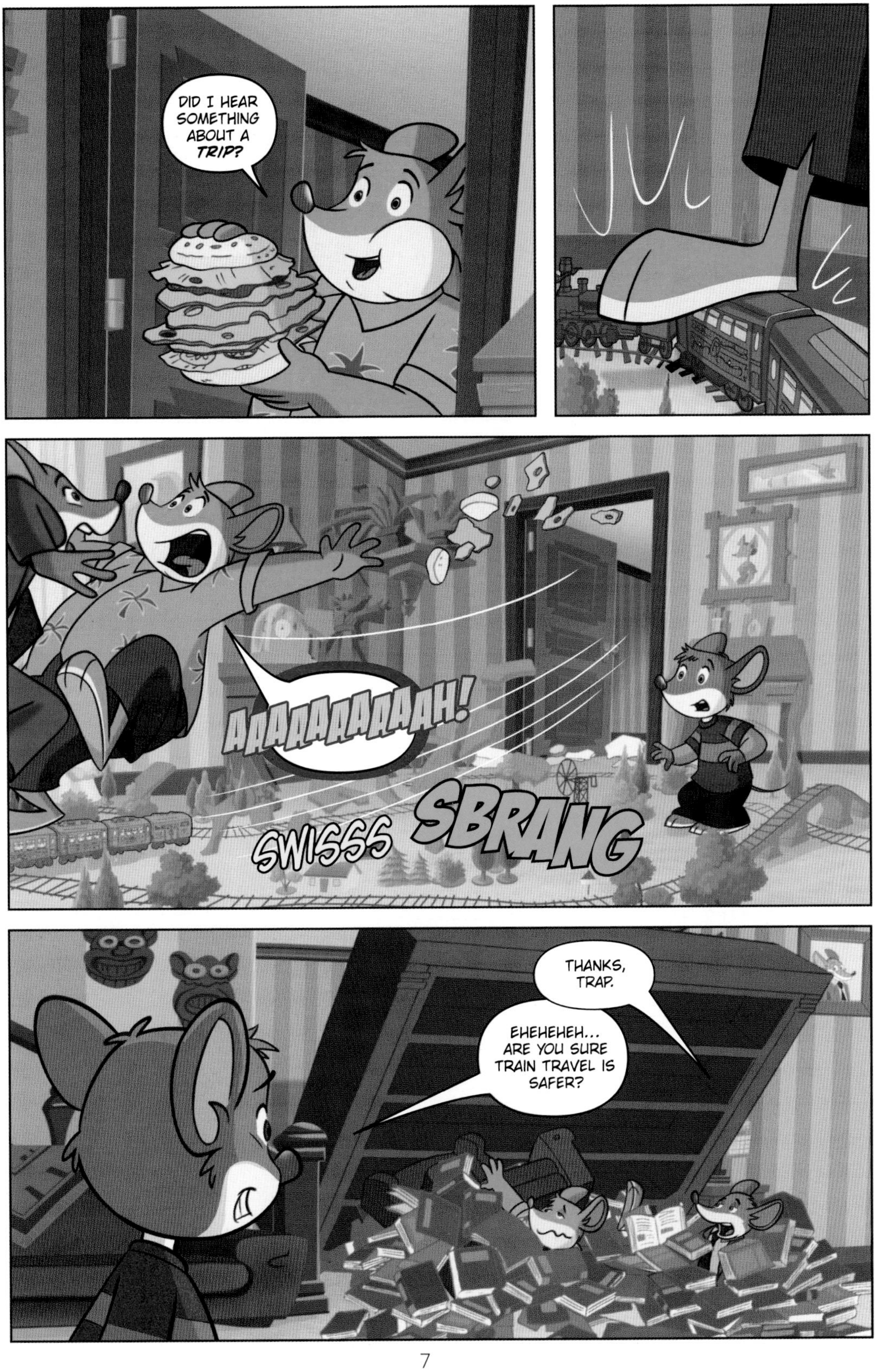
DID I HEAR SOMETHING ABOUT A TRIP?
AAAAAAAAAAH!
SWISSS
SBRANG
THANKS, TRAP.
EHEHEHEH... ARE YOU SURE TRAIN TRAVEL IS SAFER?

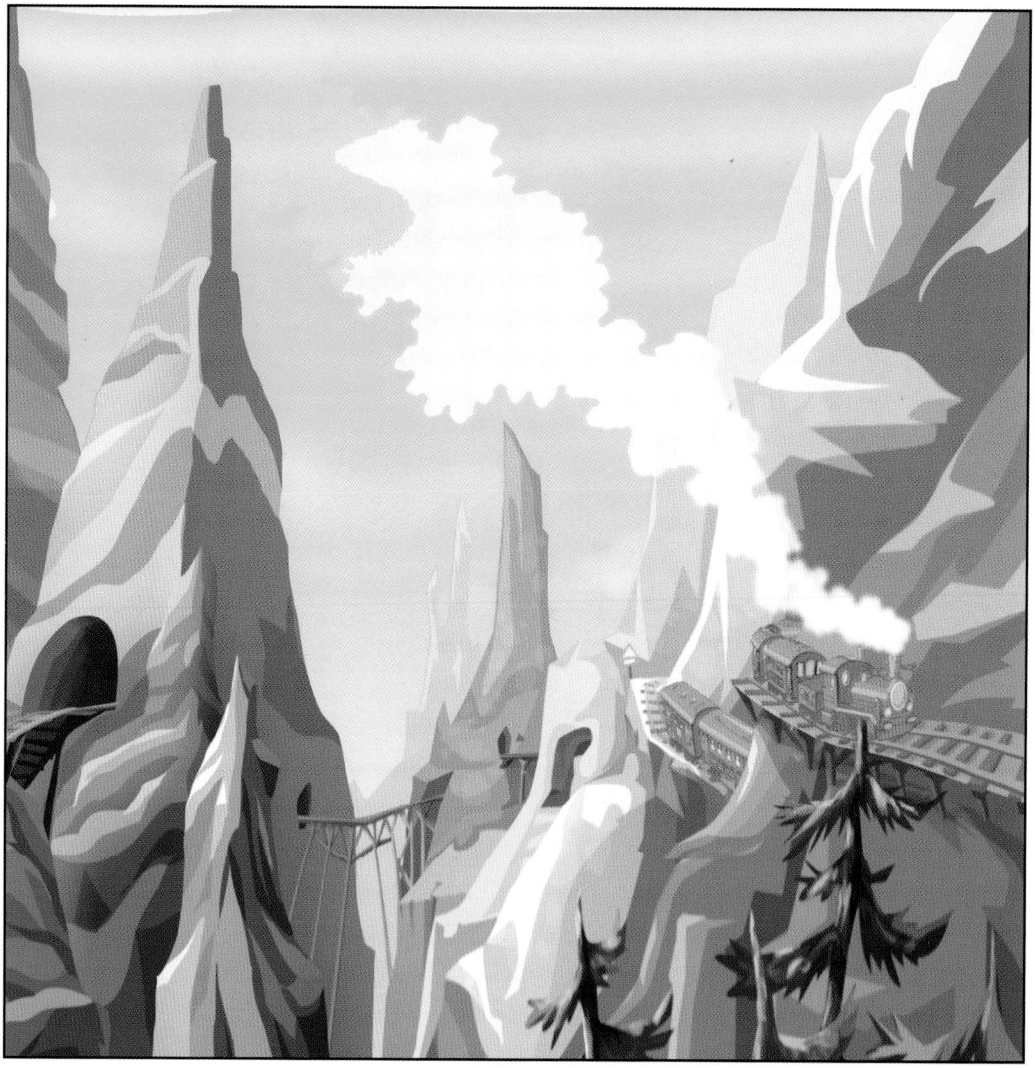

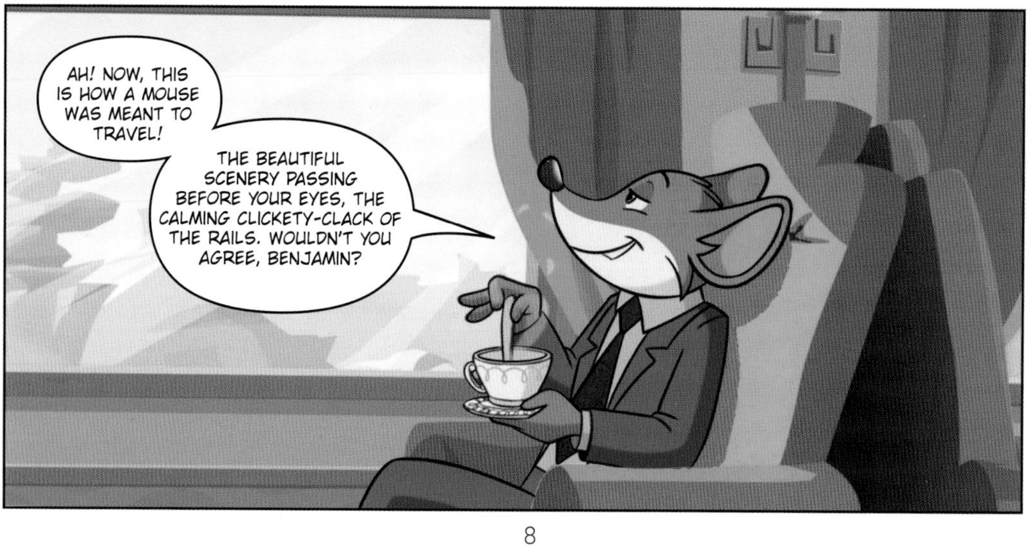
AH! NOW, THIS IS HOW A MOUSE WAS MEANT TO TRAVEL!
THE BEAUTIFUL SCENERY PASSING BEFORE YOUR EYES, THE CALMING CLICKETY-CLACK OF THE RAILS. WOULDN'T YOU AGREE, BENJAMIN?

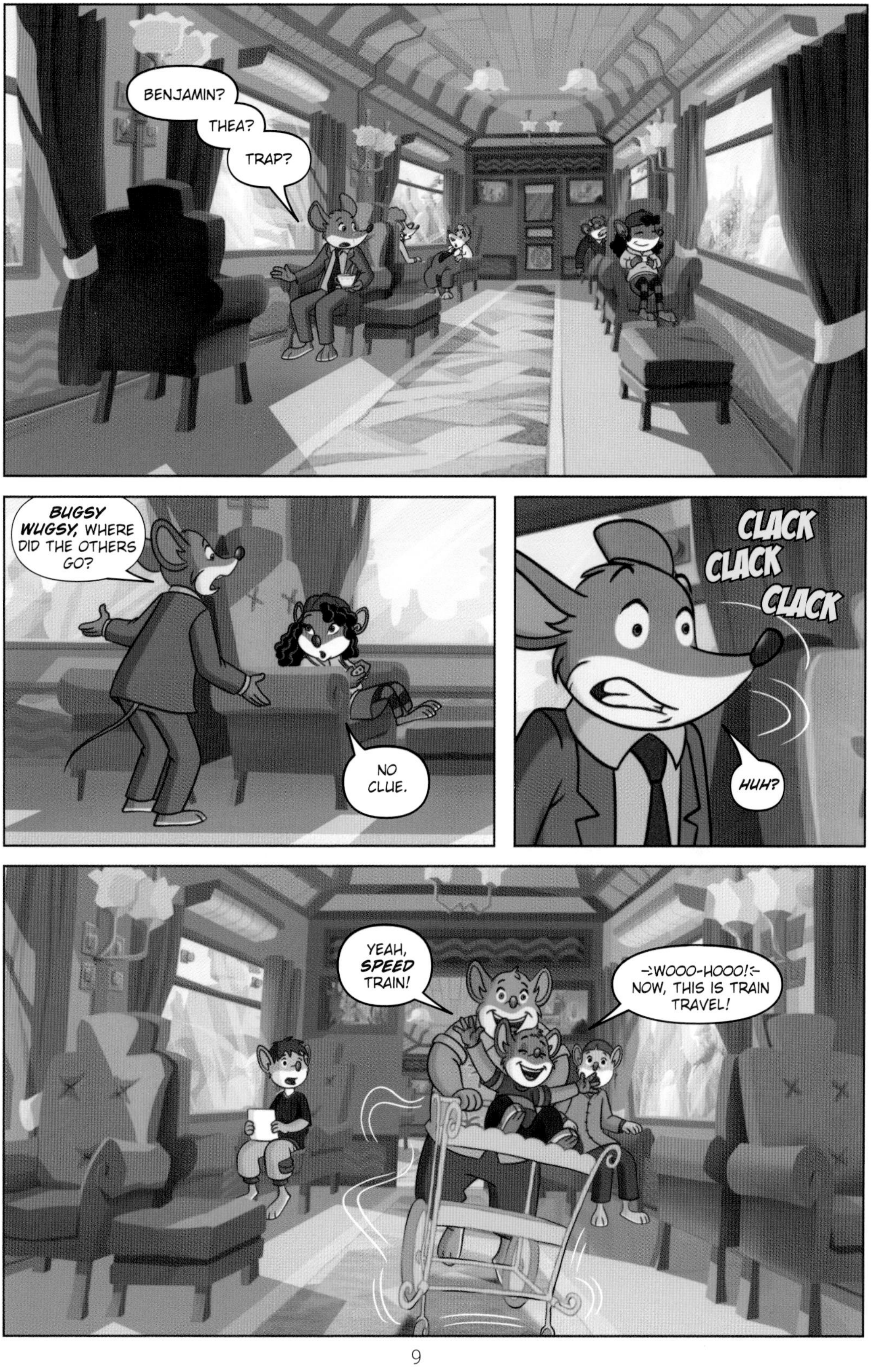
BENJAMIN?
THEA?
TRAP?
BUGSY WUGSY, WHERE DID THE OTHERS GO?
NO CLUE.
CLACK
CLACK
CLACK
HUH?
YEAH, SPEED TRAIN!
WOOO-HOOO! NOW, THIS IS TRAIN TRAVEL!

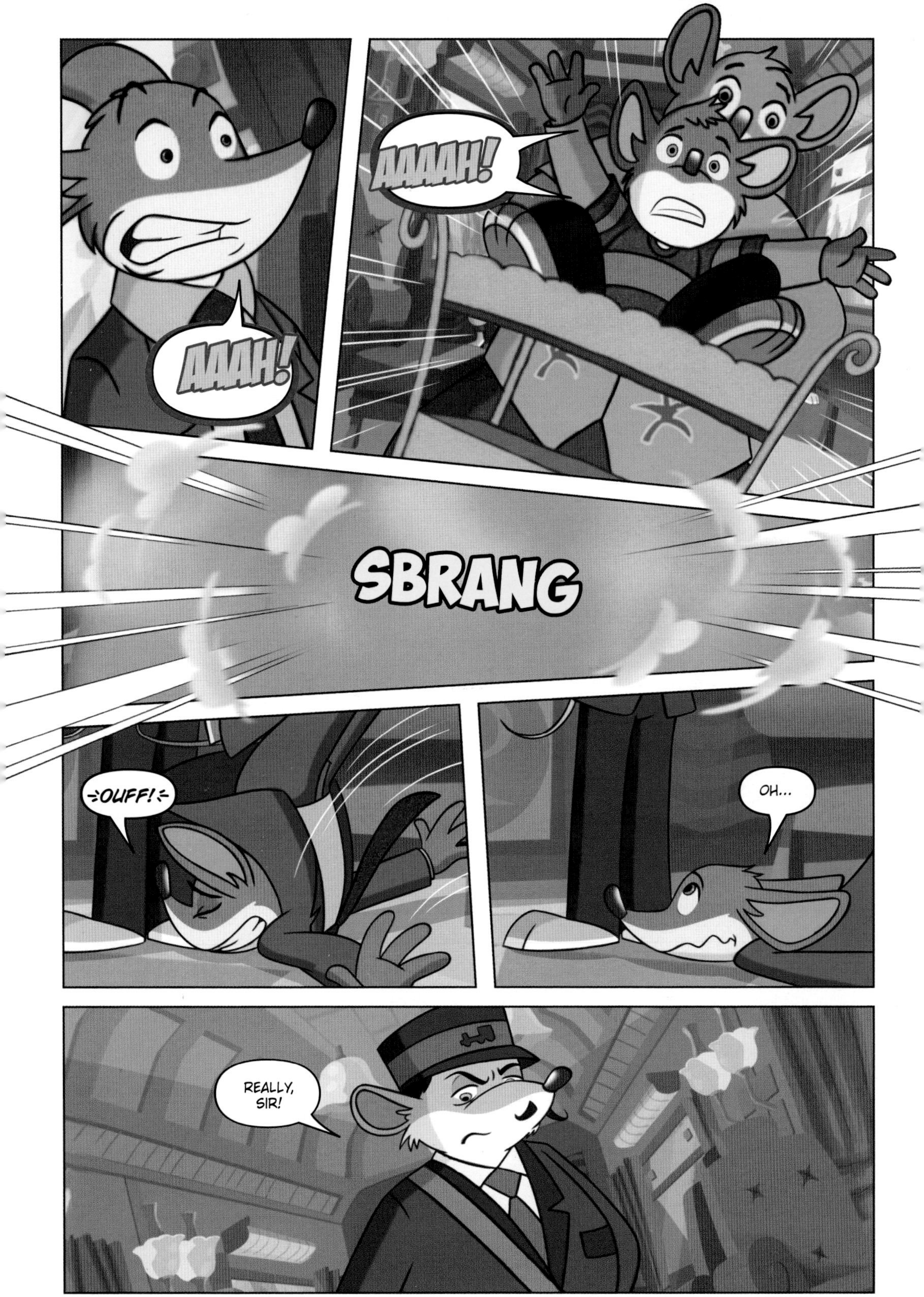
AAAH!
AAAAH!
SBRANG
OUFF!
OH...
REALLY, SIR!

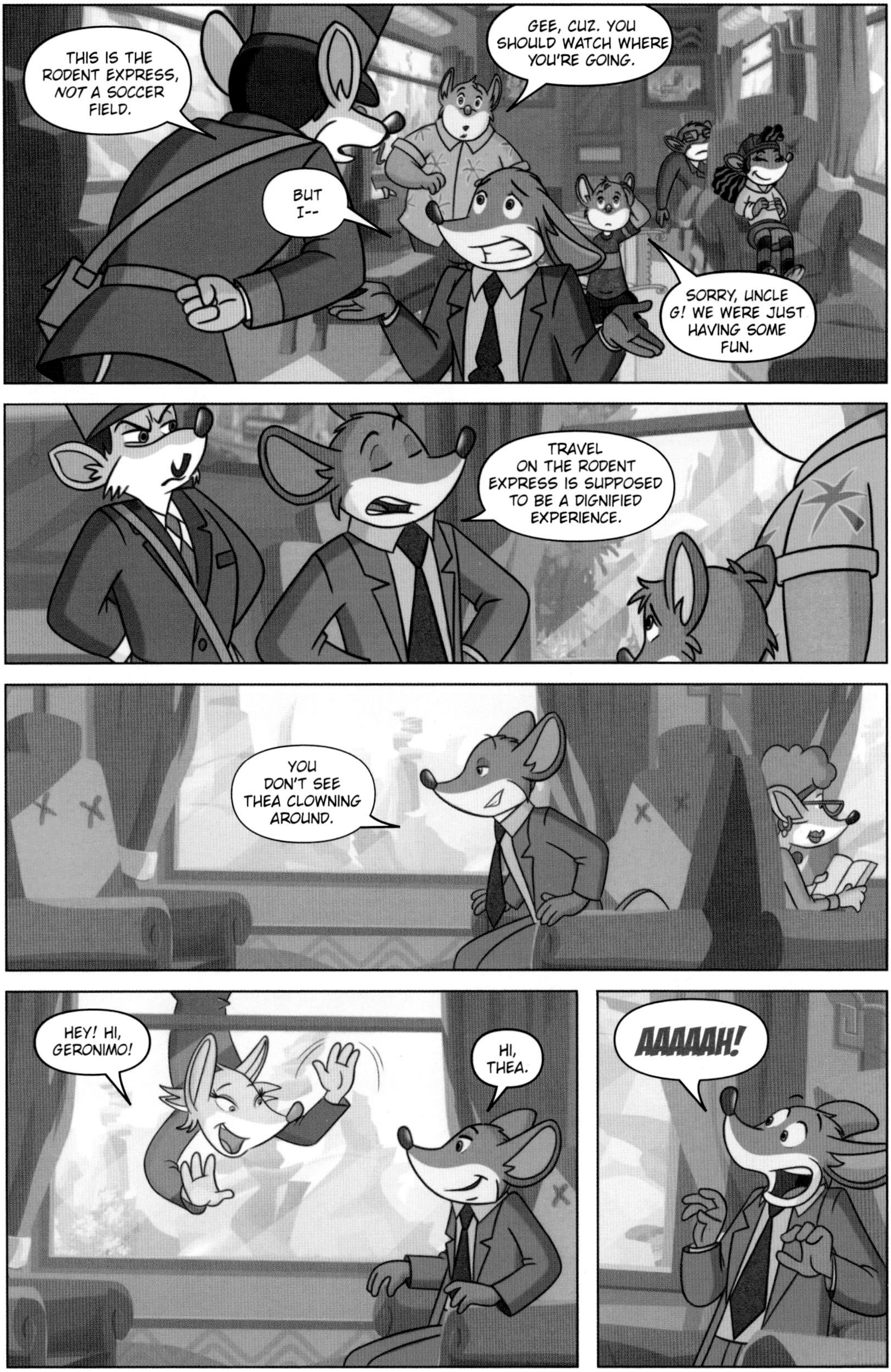
THIS IS THE RODENT EXPRESS, *NOT* A SOCCER FIELD.
GEE, CUZ. YOU SHOULD WATCH WHERE YOU'RE GOING.
BUT I--
SORRY, UNCLE G! WE WERE JUST HAVING SOME FUN.
TRAVEL ON THE RODENT EXPRESS IS SUPPOSED TO BE A DIGNIFIED EXPERIENCE.
YOU DON'T SEE THEA CLOWNING AROUND.
HEY! HI, GERONIMO!
HI, THEA.
AAAAAH!

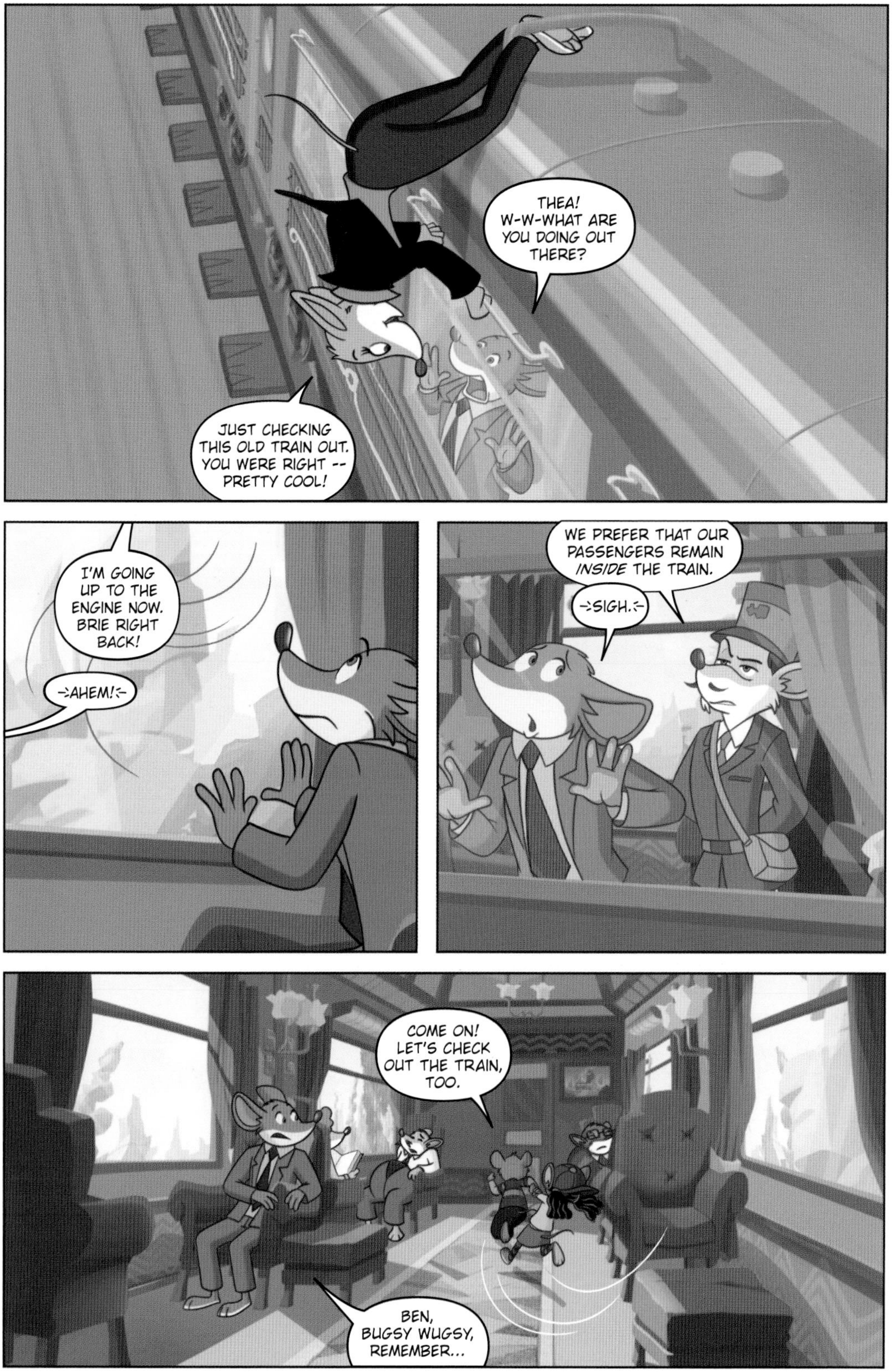
THEA! W-W-WHAT ARE YOU DOING OUT THERE?
JUST CHECKING THIS OLD TRAIN OUT. YOU WERE RIGHT -- PRETTY COOL!
I'M GOING UP TO THE ENGINE NOW. BRIE RIGHT BACK!
-AHEM!-
WE PREFER THAT OUR PASSENGERS REMAIN *INSIDE* THE TRAIN.
-SIGH.-
COME ON! LET'S CHECK OUT THE TRAIN, TOO.
BEN, BUGSY WUGSY, REMEMBER...

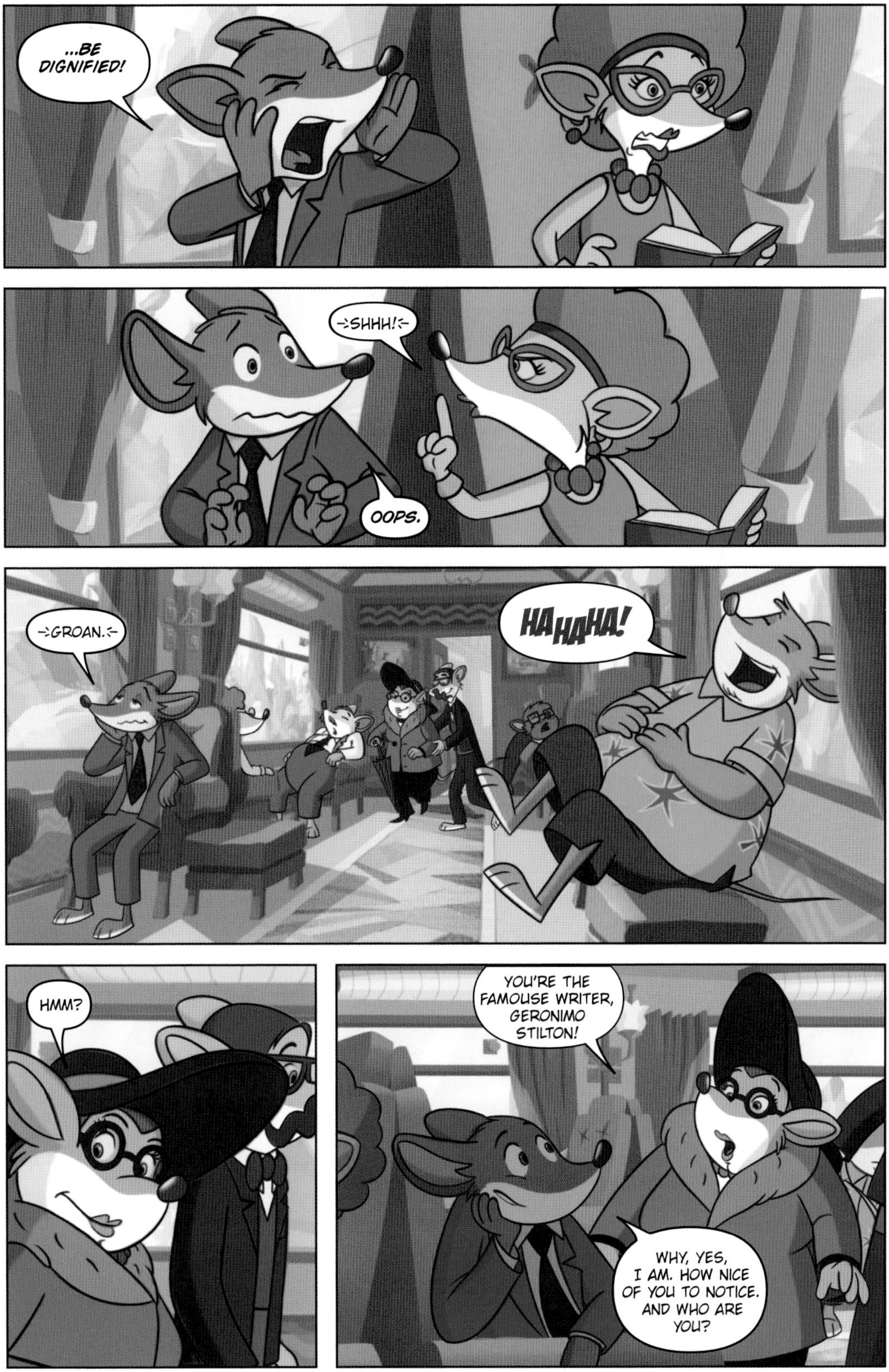
...BE DIGNIFIED!
SHHH!
OOPS.
GROAN.
HAHAHA!
HMM?
YOU'RE THE FAMOUSE WRITER, GERONIMO STILTON!
WHY, YES, I AM. HOW NICE OF YOU TO NOTICE. AND WHO ARE YOU?

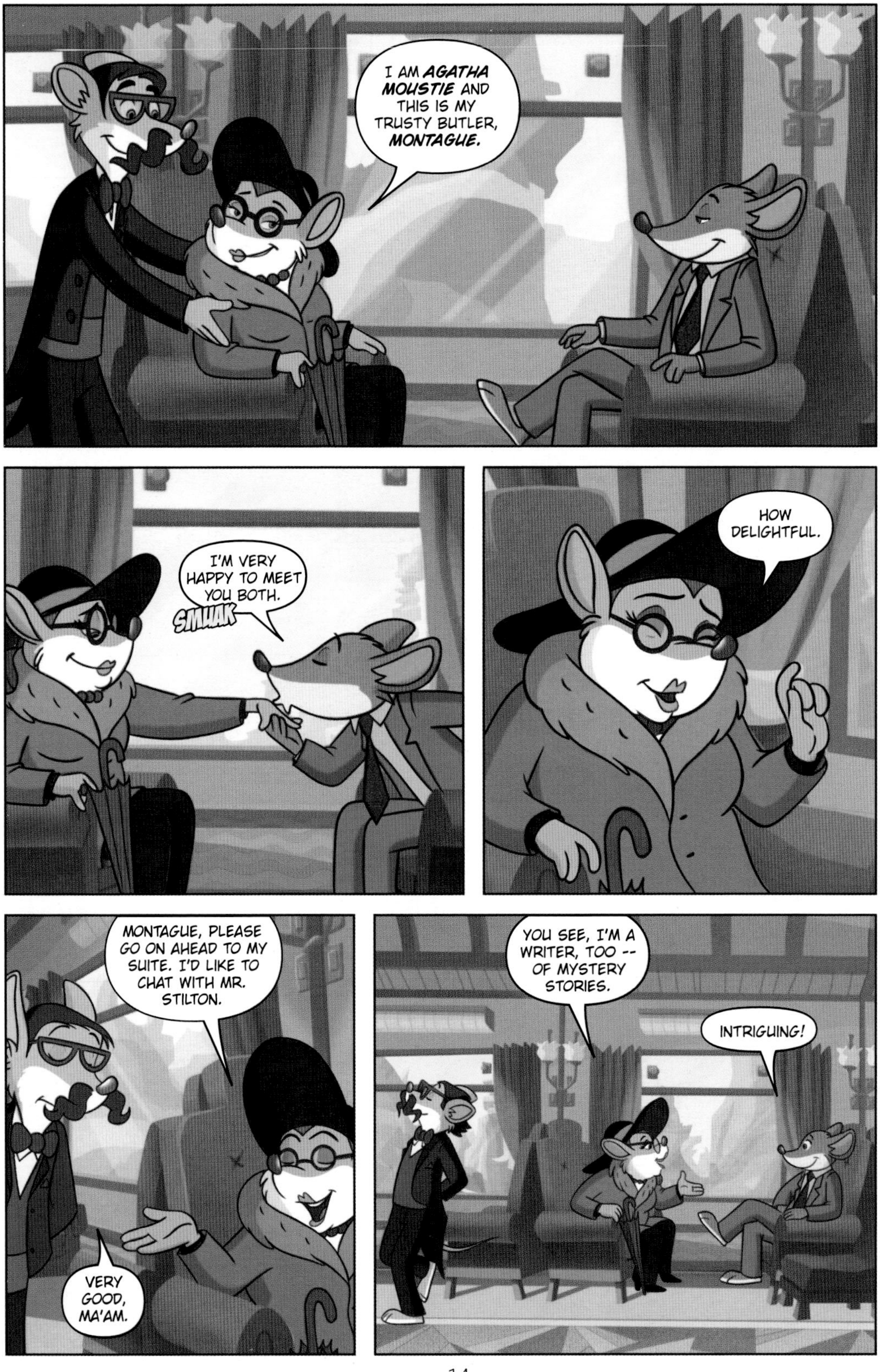
I AM ***AGATHA MOUSTIE*** AND THIS IS MY TRUSTY BUTLER, ***MONTAGUE.***
I'M VERY HAPPY TO MEET YOU BOTH.
SMUAK
HOW DELIGHTFUL.
MONTAGUE, PLEASE GO ON AHEAD TO MY SUITE. I'D LIKE TO CHAT WITH MR. STILTON.
VERY GOOD, MA'AM.
YOU SEE, I'M A WRITER, TOO -- OF MYSTERY STORIES.
INTRIGUING!

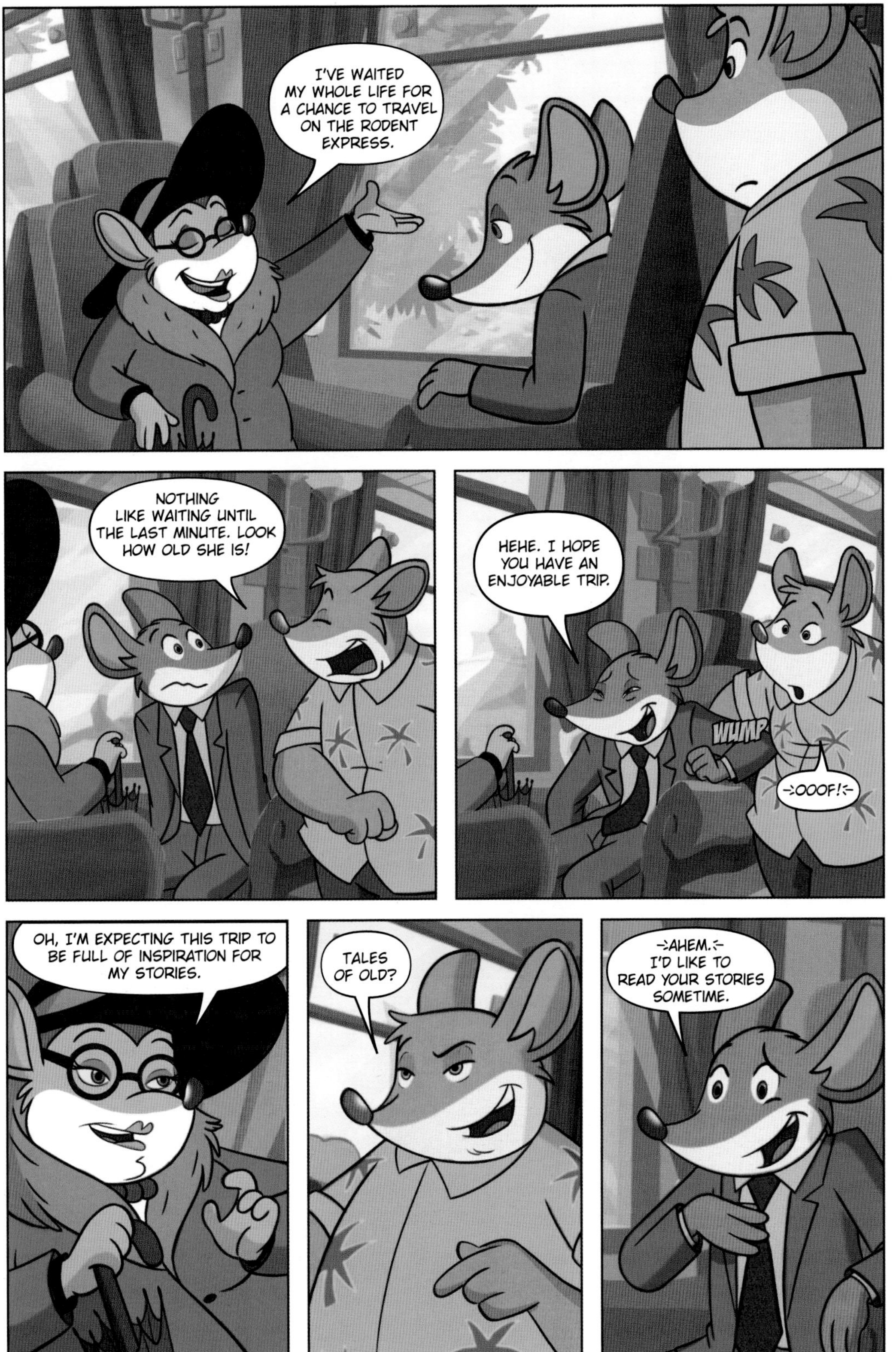
I'VE WAITED MY WHOLE LIFE FOR A CHANCE TO TRAVEL ON THE RODENT EXPRESS.
NOTHING LIKE WAITING UNTIL THE LAST MINUTE. LOOK HOW OLD SHE IS!
HEHE. I HOPE YOU HAVE AN ENJOYABLE TRIP.
WUMP
OOOF!
OH, I'M EXPECTING THIS TRIP TO BE FULL OF INSPIRATION FOR MY STORIES.
TALES OF OLD?
AHEM.
I'D LIKE TO READ YOUR STORIES SOMETIME.

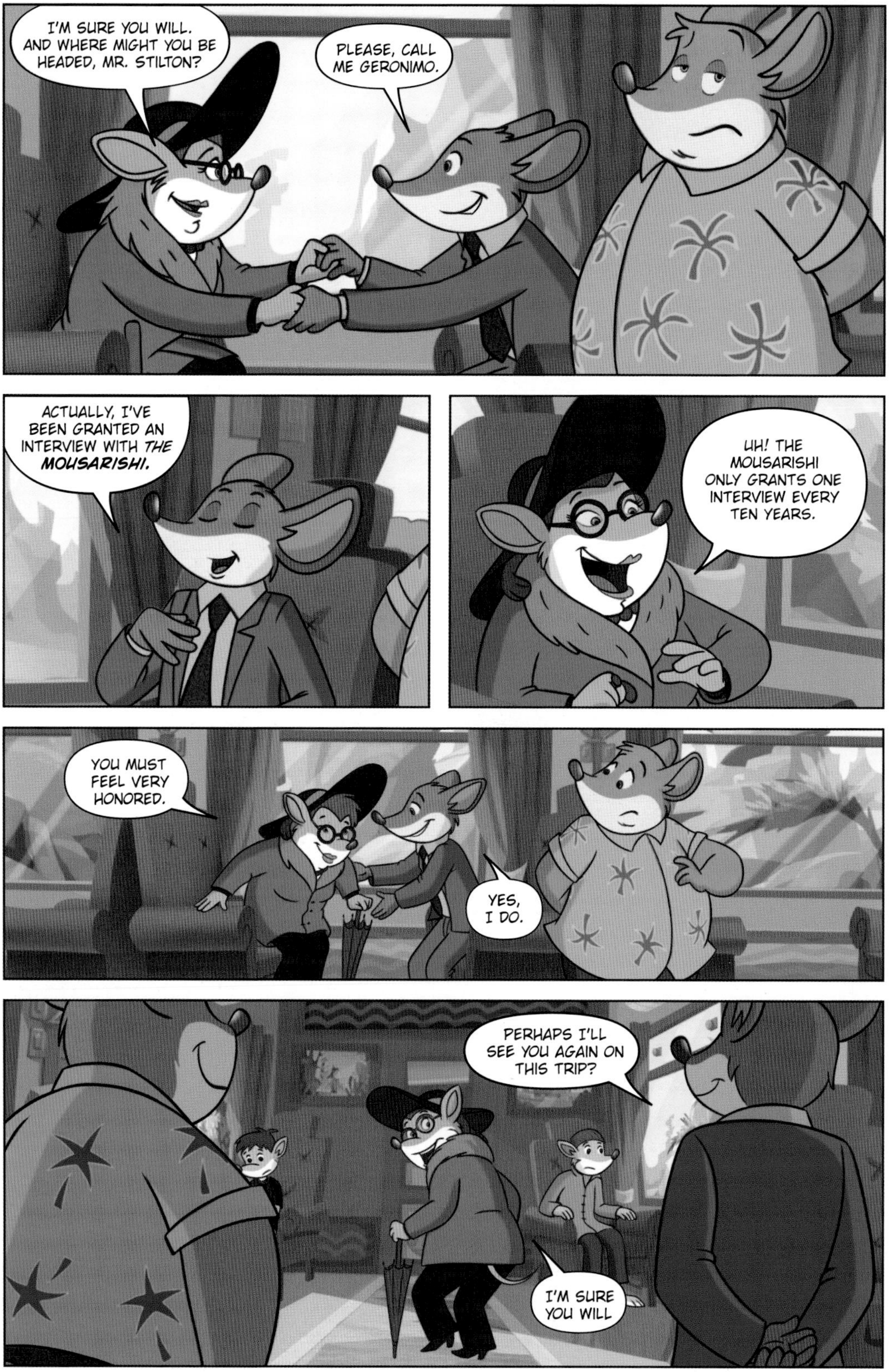
I'M SURE YOU WILL. AND WHERE MIGHT YOU BE HEADED, MR. STILTON?
PLEASE, CALL ME GERONIMO.
ACTUALLY, I'VE BEEN GRANTED AN INTERVIEW WITH *THE* ***MOUSARISHI.***
UH! THE MOUSARISHI ONLY GRANTS ONE INTERVIEW EVERY TEN YEARS.
YOU MUST FEEL VERY HONORED.
YES, I DO.
PERHAPS I'LL SEE YOU AGAIN ON THIS TRIP?
I'M SURE YOU WILL

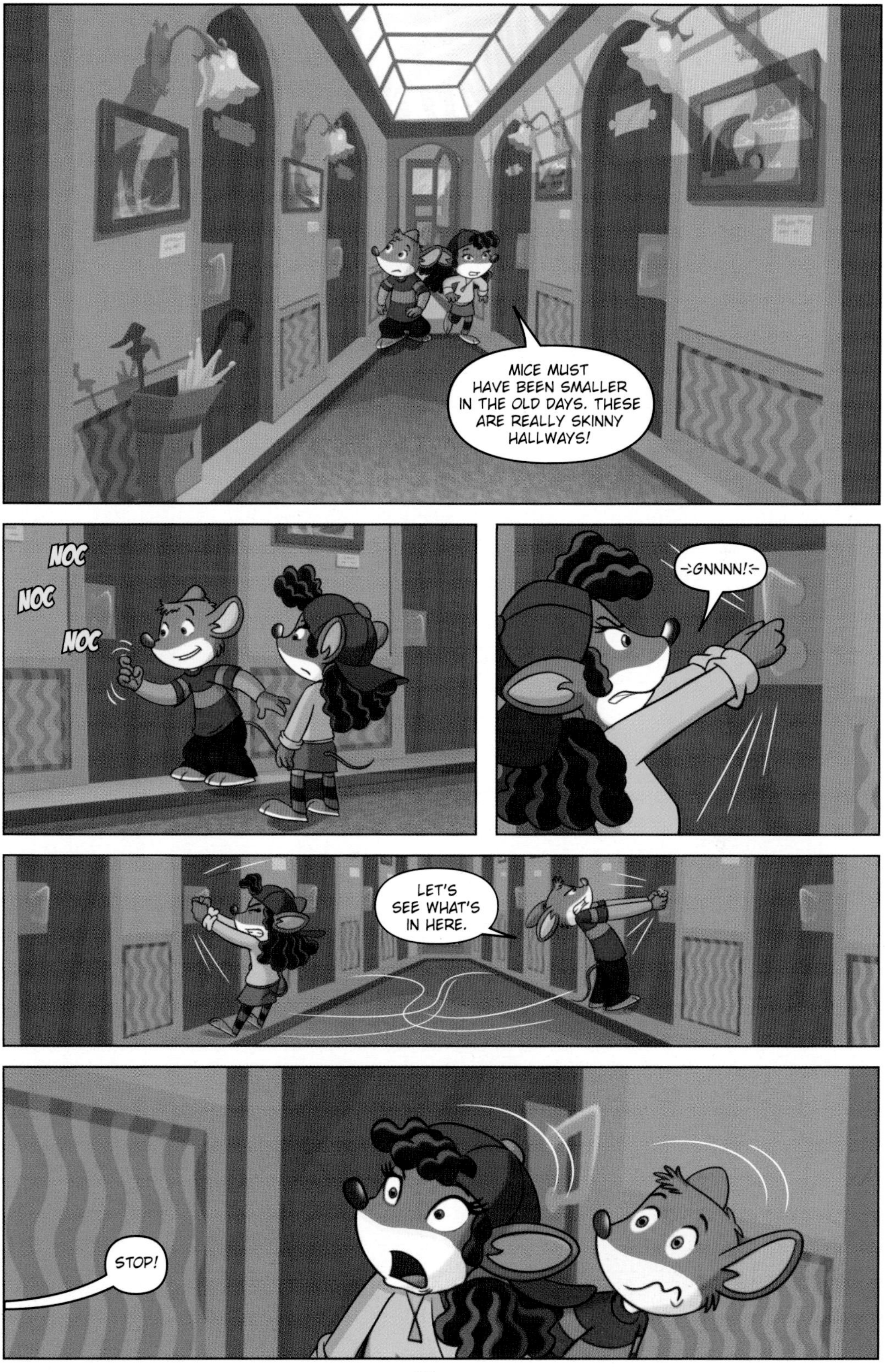
MICE MUST HAVE BEEN SMALLER IN THE OLD DAYS. THESE ARE REALLY SKINNY HALLWAYS!
NOC
NOC
NOC
GNNNN!
LET'S SEE WHAT'S IN HERE.
STOP!

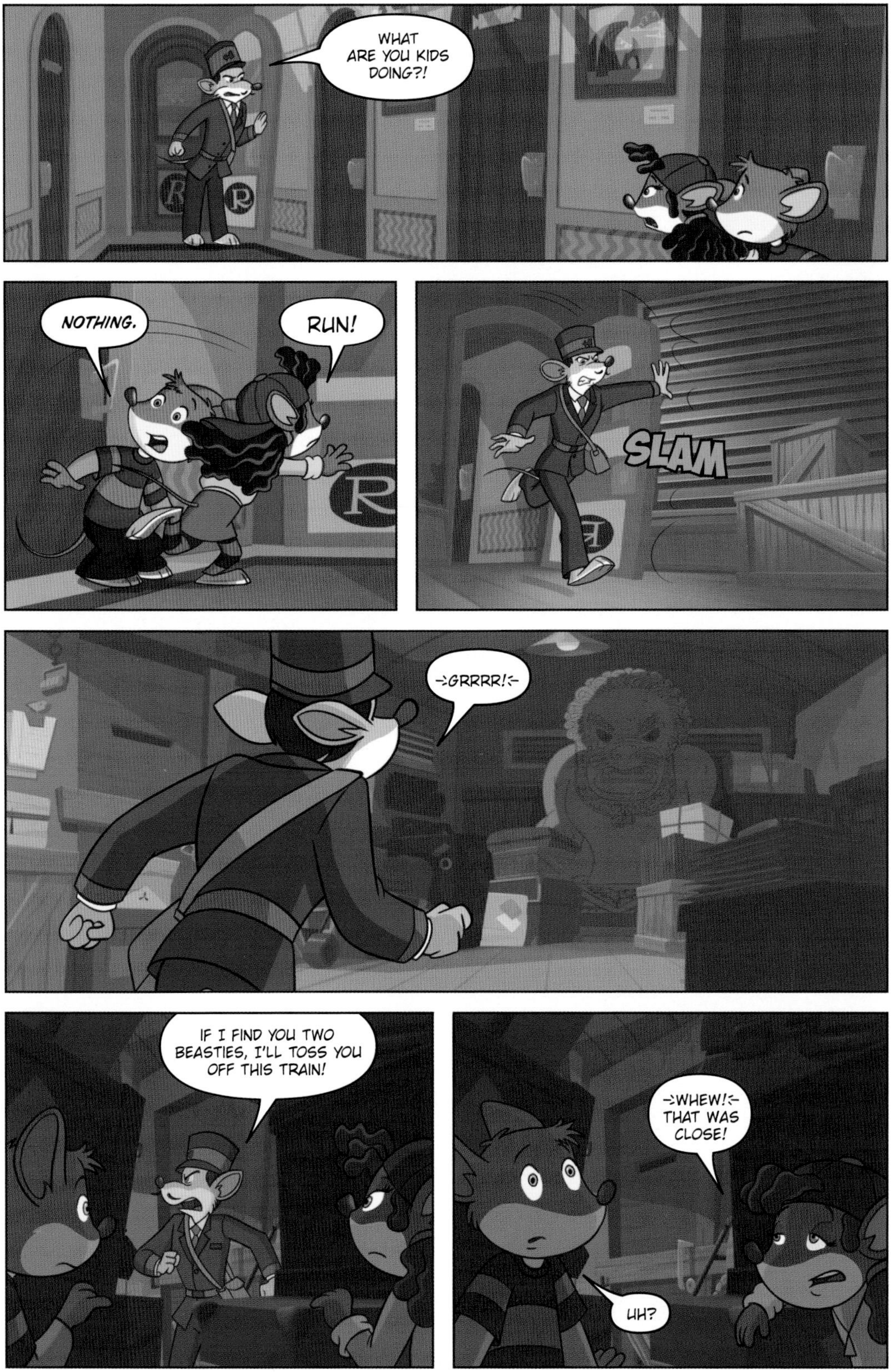
WHAT ARE YOU KIDS DOING?!
NOTHING.
RUN!
SLAM
-GRRRR!-
IF I FIND YOU TWO BEASTIES, I'LL TOSS YOU OFF THIS TRAIN!
-WHEW!- THAT WAS CLOSE!
UH?

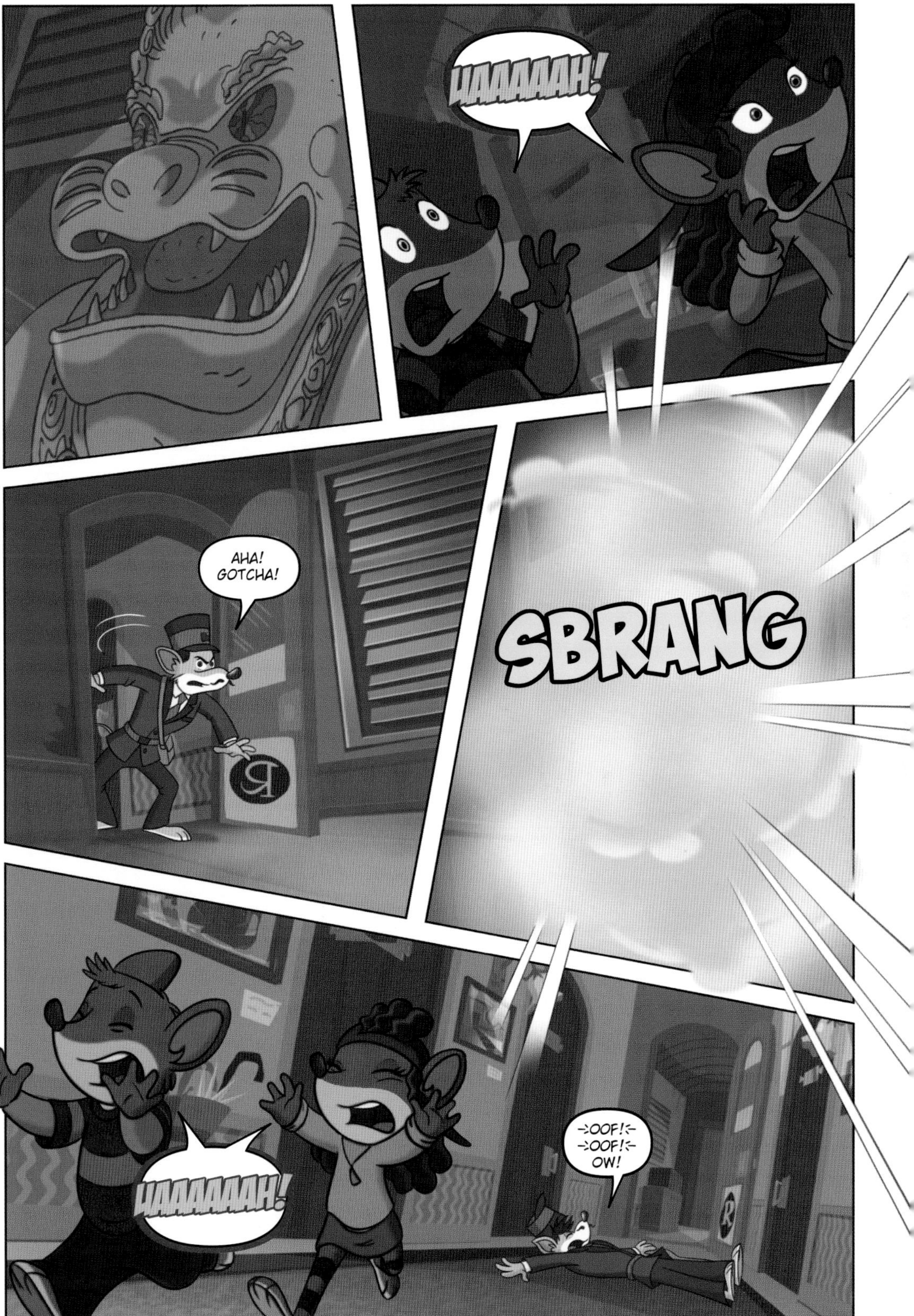
UAAAAAH!
AHA! GOTCHA!
SBRANG
UAAAAAAH!
OOF! OOF! OW!

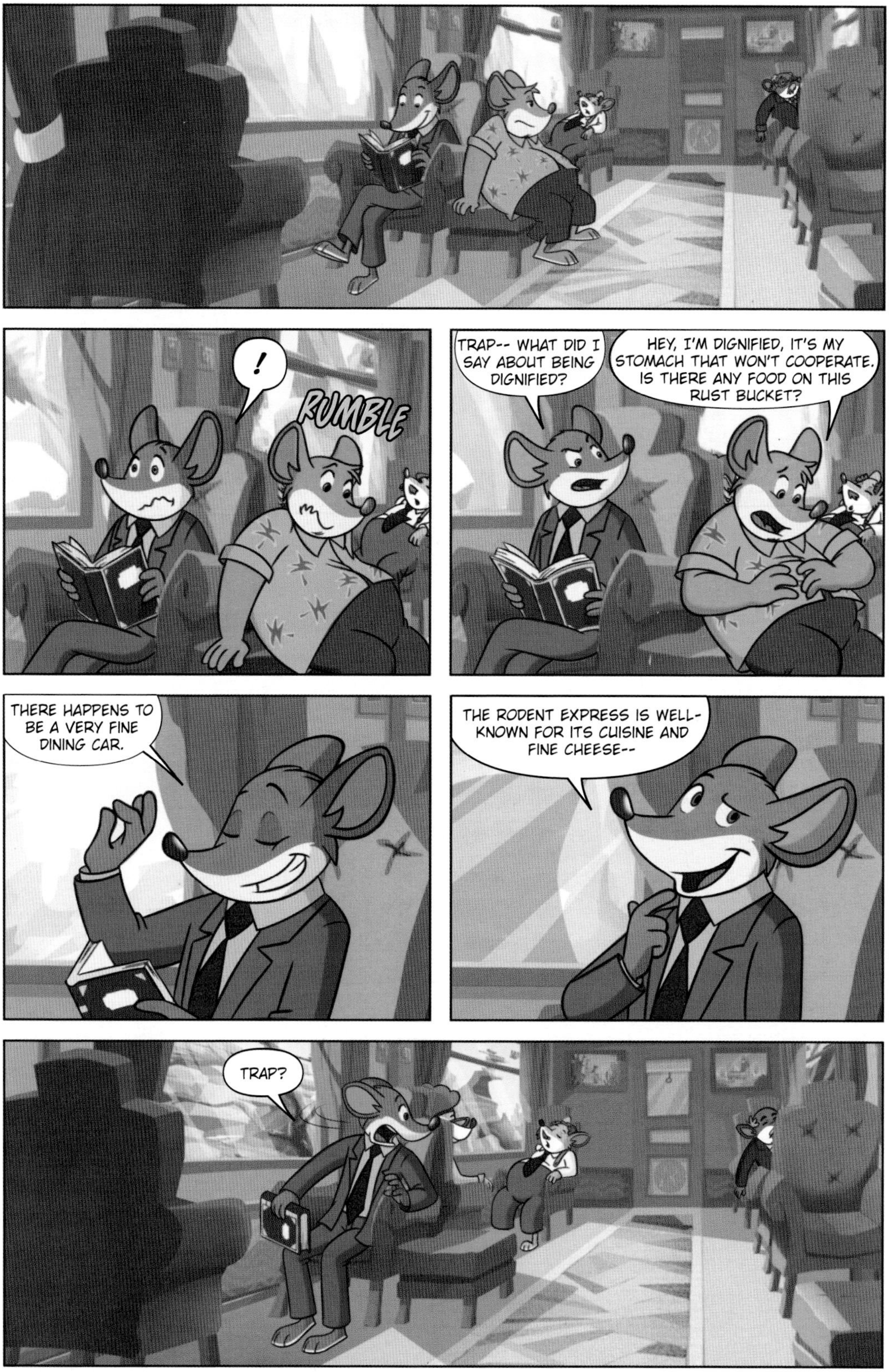
!
RUMBLE
TRAP-- WHAT DID I SAY ABOUT BEING DIGNIFIED?
HEY, I'M DIGNIFIED, IT'S MY STOMACH THAT WON'T COOPERATE. IS THERE ANY FOOD ON THIS RUST BUCKET?
THERE HAPPENS TO BE A VERY FINE DINING CAR.
THE RODENT EXPRESS IS WELL-KNOWN FOR ITS CUISINE AND FINE CHEESE--
TRAP?

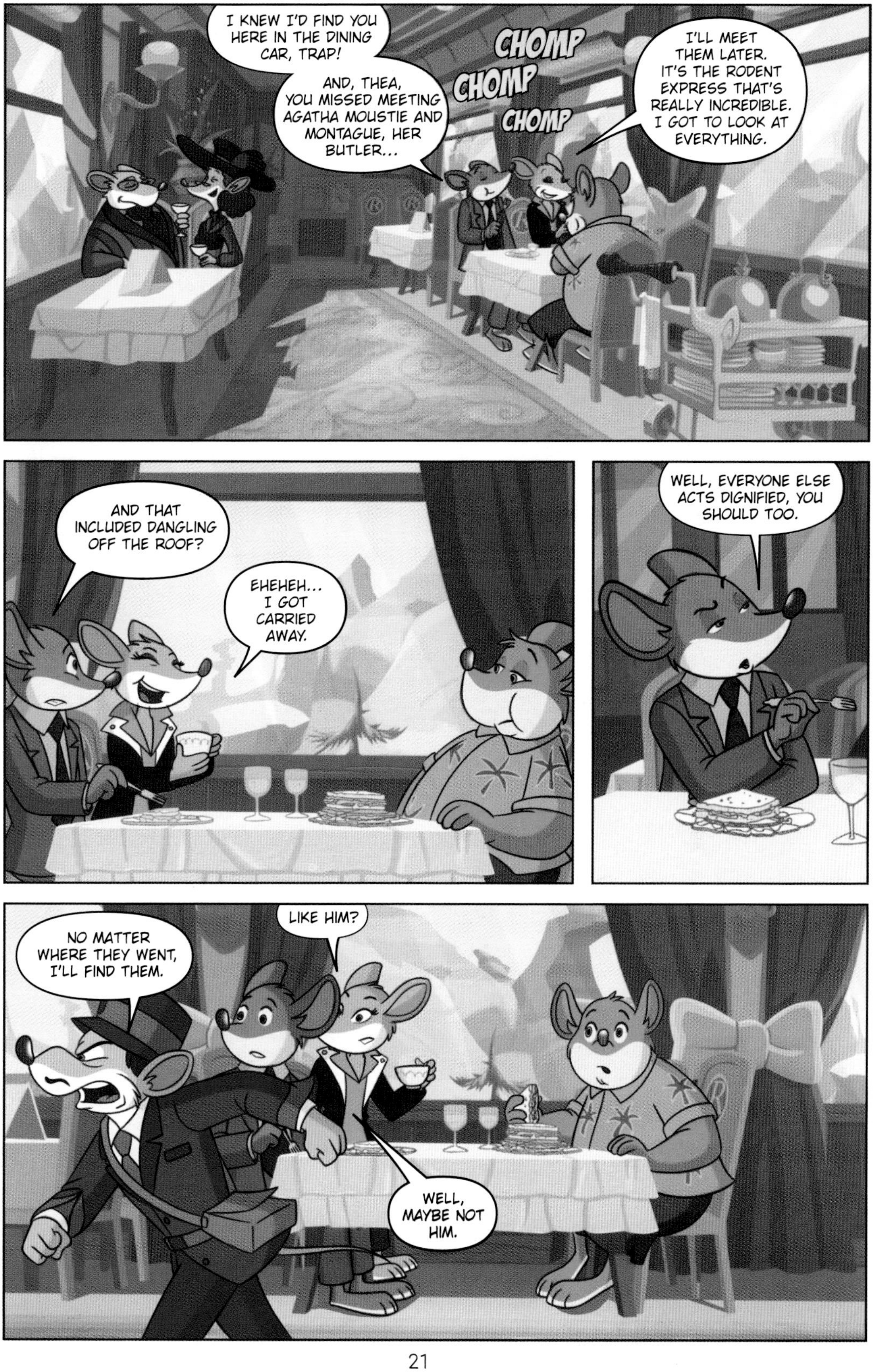
I KNEW I'D FIND YOU HERE IN THE DINING CAR, TRAP!
AND, THEA, YOU MISSED MEETING AGATHA MOUSTIE AND MONTAGUE, HER BUTLER...
CHOMP
CHOMP
CHOMP
I'LL MEET THEM LATER. IT'S THE RODENT EXPRESS THAT'S REALLY INCREDIBLE. I GOT TO LOOK AT EVERYTHING.
AND THAT INCLUDED DANGLING OFF THE ROOF?
EHEHEH... I GOT CARRIED AWAY.
WELL, EVERYONE ELSE ACTS DIGNIFIED, YOU SHOULD TOO.
NO MATTER WHERE THEY WENT, I'LL FIND THEM.
LIKE HIM?
WELL, MAYBE NOT HIM.

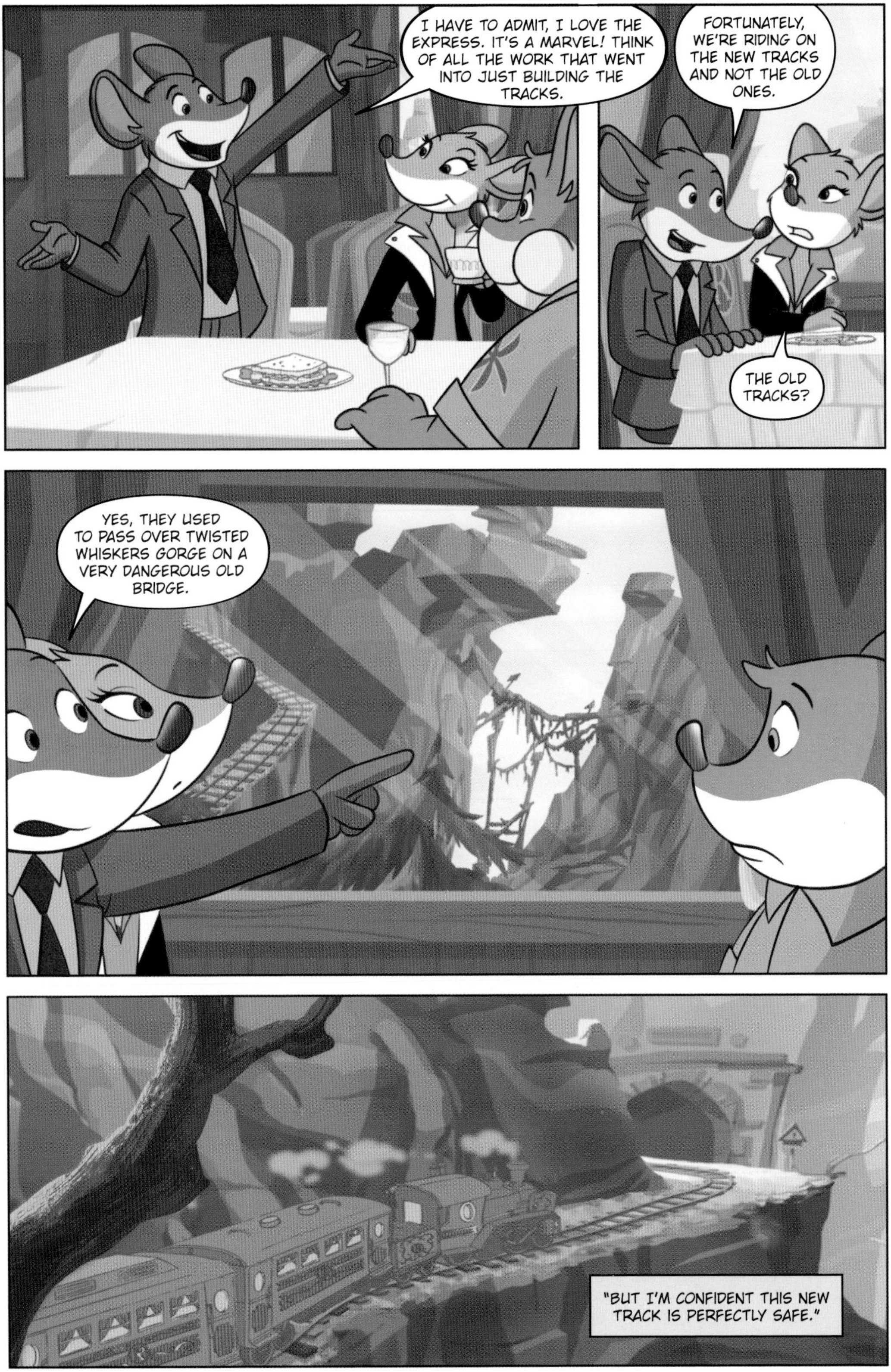
I HAVE TO ADMIT, I LOVE THE EXPRESS. IT'S A MARVEL! THINK OF ALL THE WORK THAT WENT INTO JUST BUILDING THE TRACKS.
FORTUNATELY, WE'RE RIDING ON THE NEW TRACKS AND NOT THE OLD ONES.
THE OLD TRACKS?
YES, THEY USED TO PASS OVER TWISTED WHISKERS GORGE ON A VERY DANGEROUS OLD BRIDGE.
"BUT I'M CONFIDENT THIS NEW TRACK IS PERFECTLY SAFE."

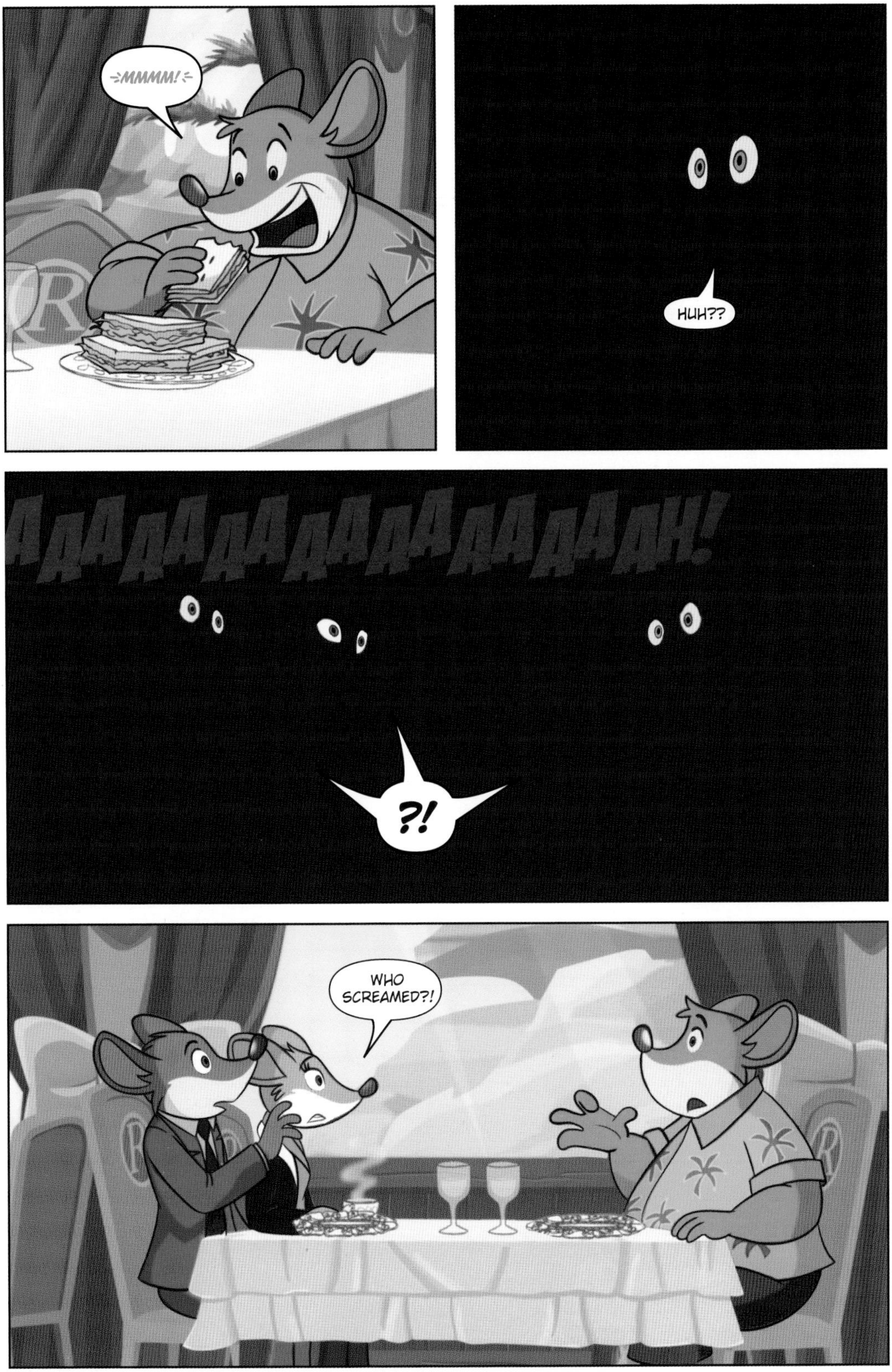
MMMM!
HUH??
AAAAAAAAAAAAAAAAAH!
?!
WHO SCREAMED?!

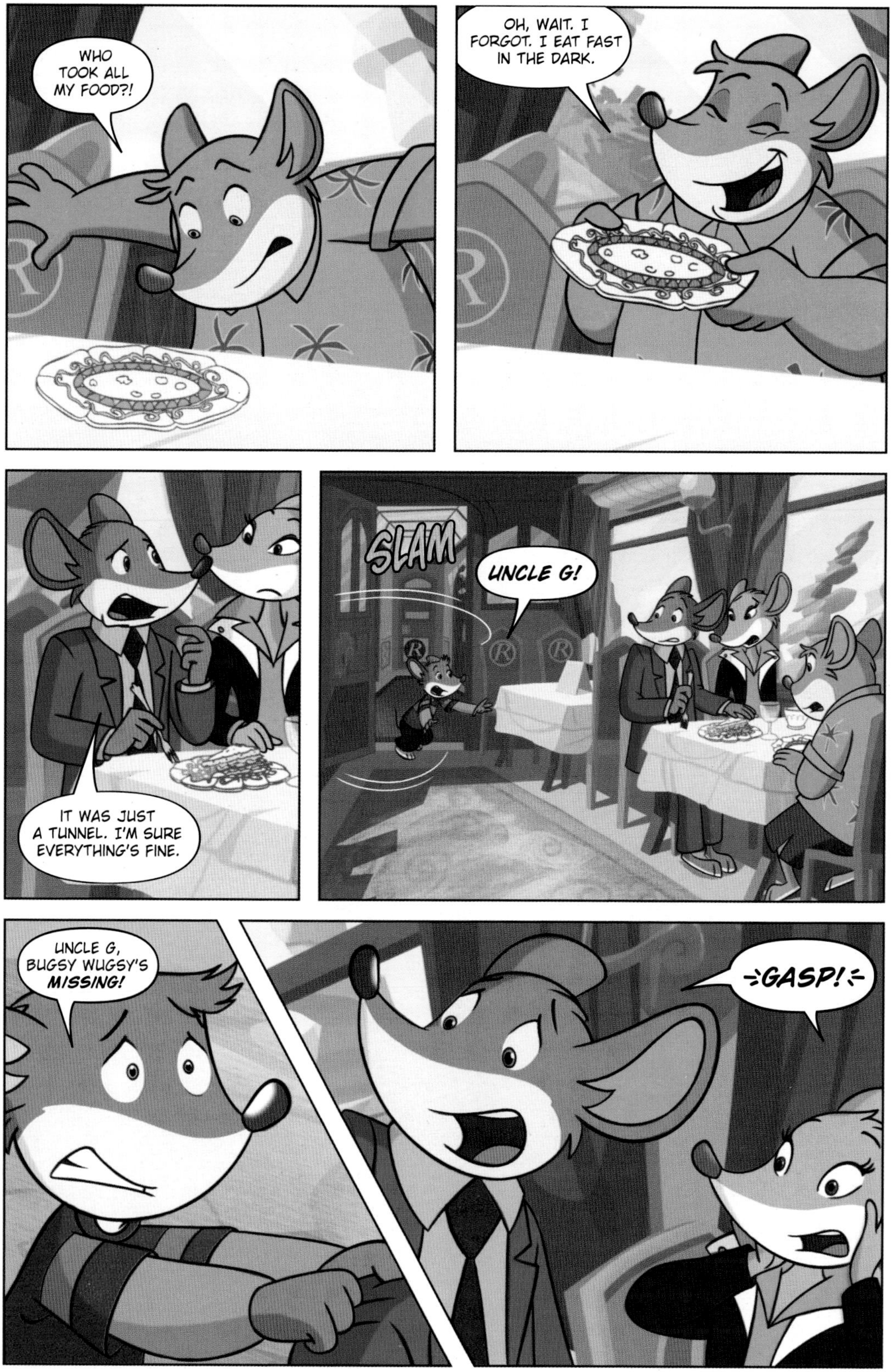
WHO TOOK ALL MY FOOD?!
OH, WAIT. I FORGOT. I EAT FAST IN THE DARK.
IT WAS JUST A TUNNEL. I'M SURE EVERYTHING'S FINE.
SLAM
UNCLE G!
UNCLE G, BUGSY WUGSY'S MISSING!
GASP!

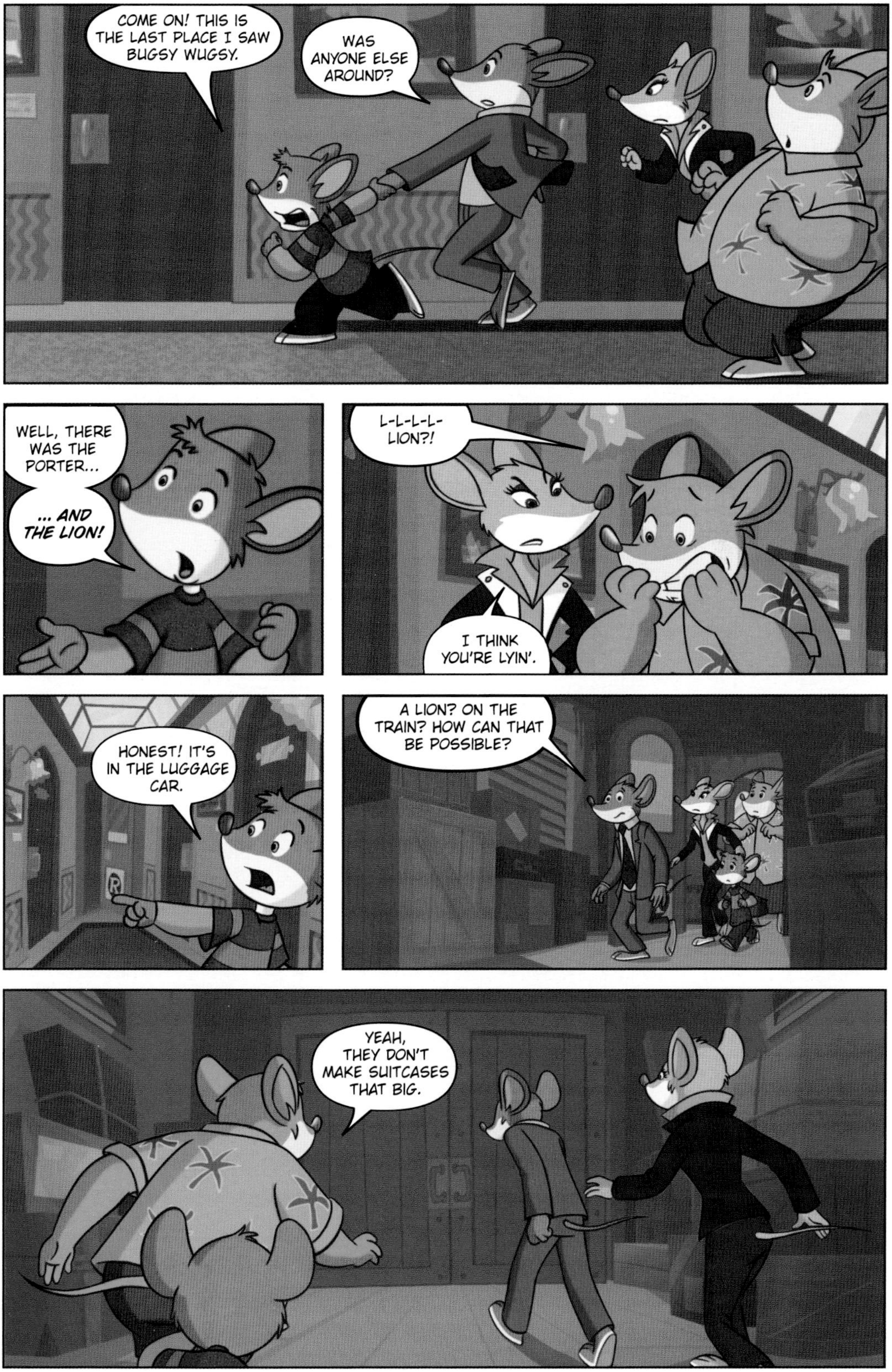
COME ON! THIS IS THE LAST PLACE I SAW BUGSY WUGSY.
WAS ANYONE ELSE AROUND?
WELL, THERE WAS THE PORTER...
... AND THE LION!
L-L-L-L-LION?!
I THINK YOU'RE LYIN'.
HONEST! IT'S IN THE LUGGAGE CAR.
A LION? ON THE TRAIN? HOW CAN THAT BE POSSIBLE?
YEAH, THEY DON'T MAKE SUITCASES THAT BIG.

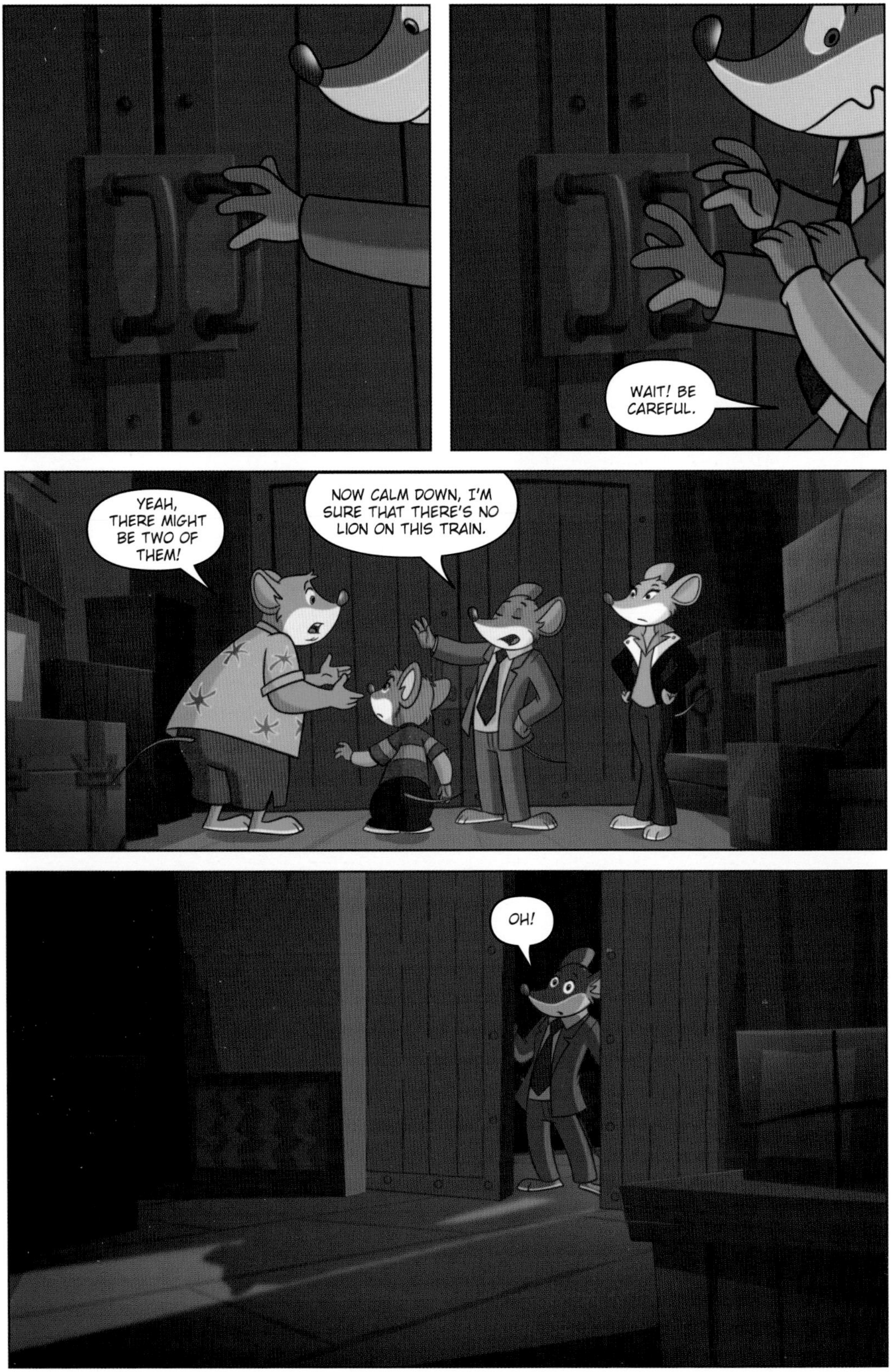

WAIT! BE CAREFUL.
YEAH, THERE MIGHT BE TWO OF THEM!
NOW CALM DOWN, I'M SURE THAT THERE'S NO LION ON THIS TRAIN.
OH!

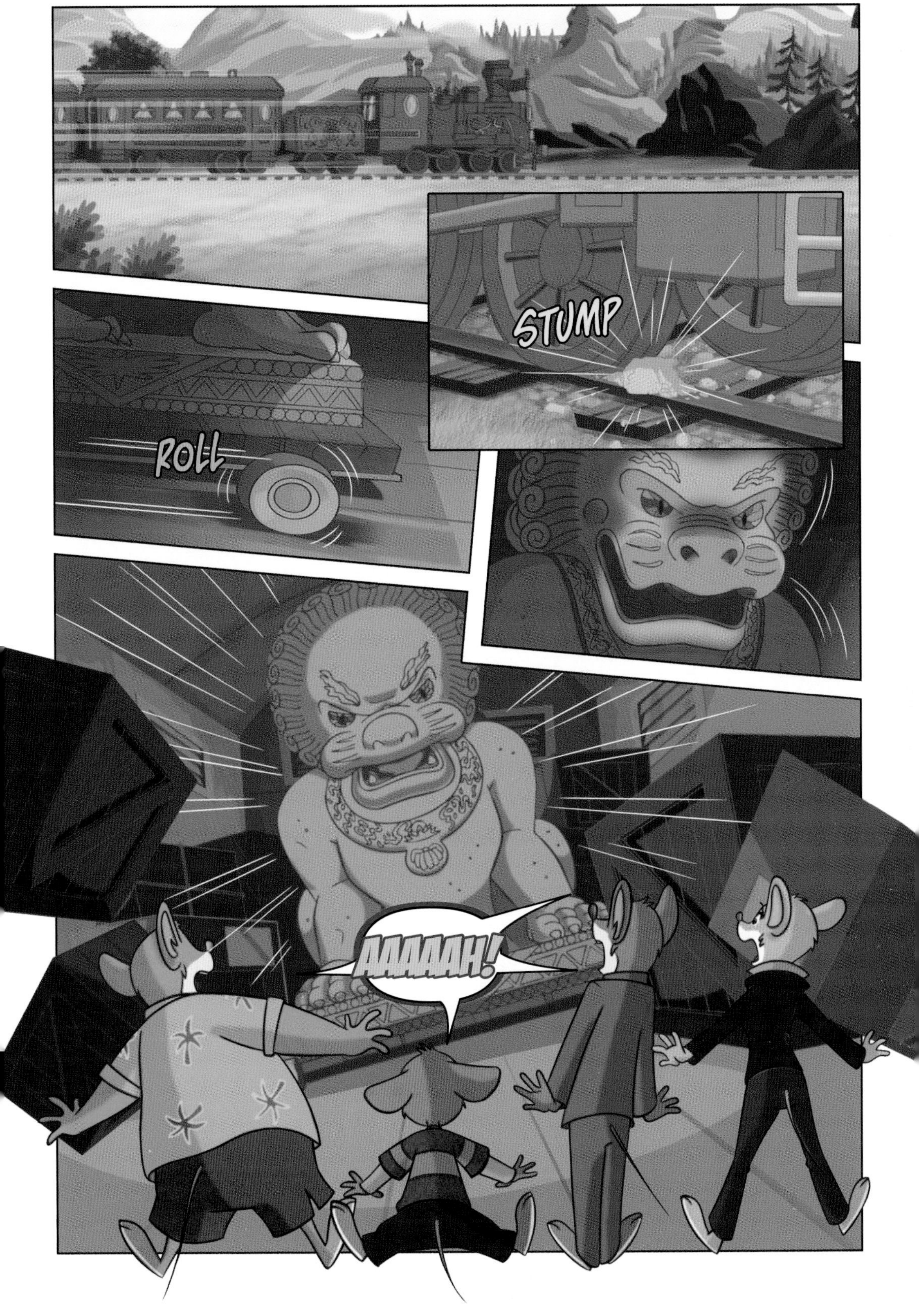
STUMP
ROLL
AAAAAH!

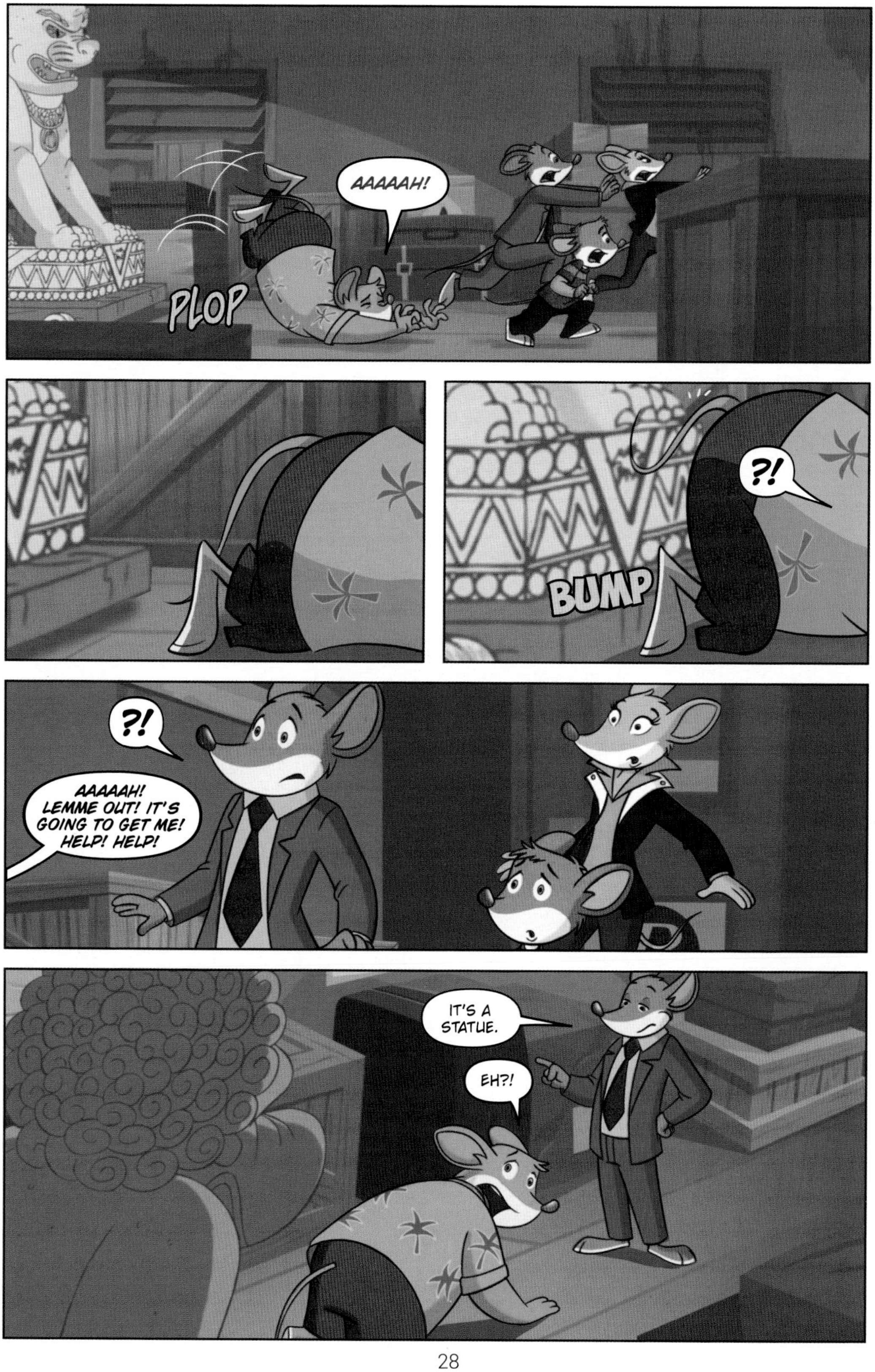
AAAAAH!
PLOP
BUMP
?!
?!
AAAAAH! LEMME OUT! IT'S GOING TO GET ME! HELP! HELP!
IT'S A STATUE.
EH?!

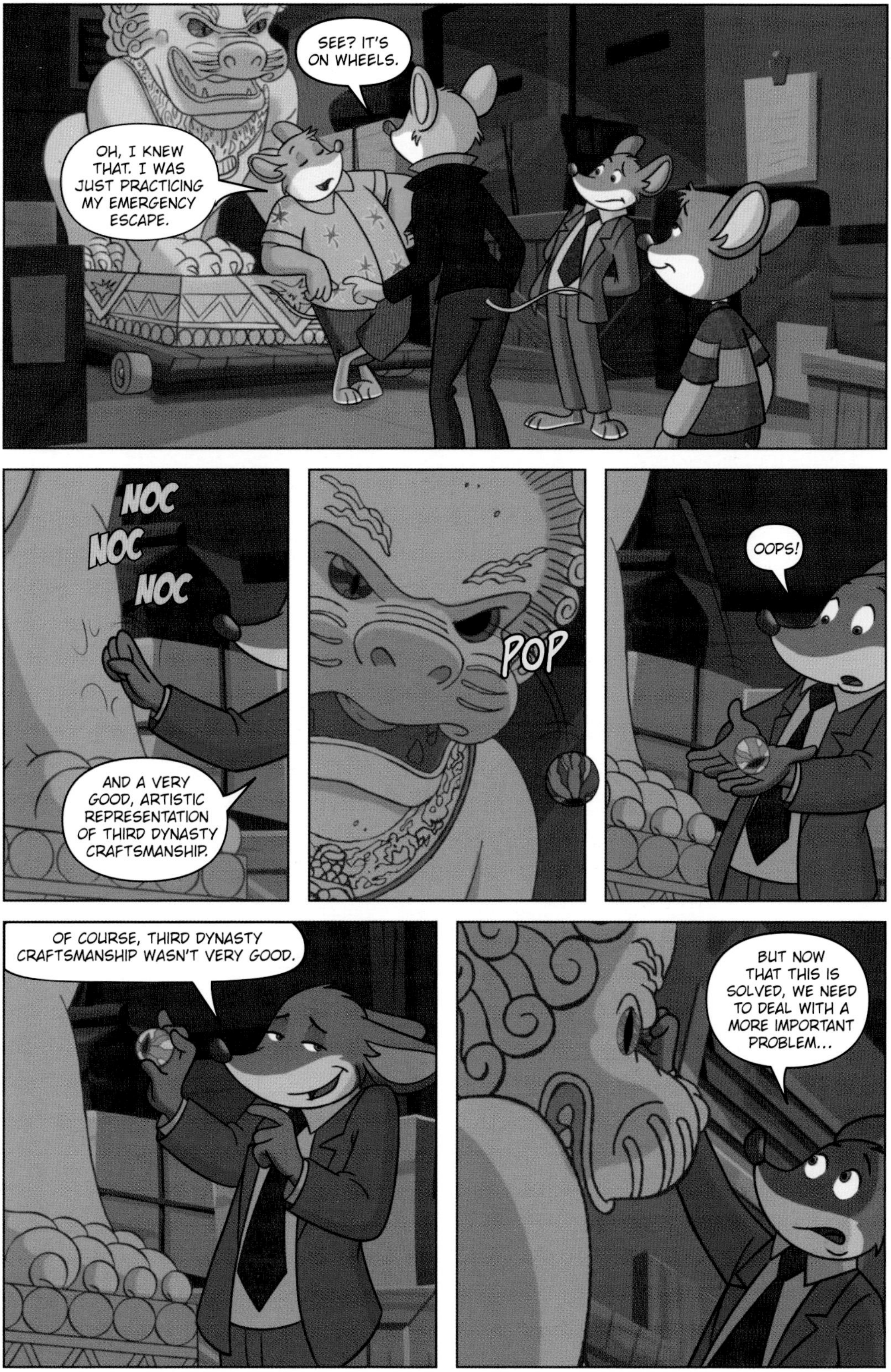
SEE? IT'S ON WHEELS.
OH, I KNEW THAT. I WAS JUST PRACTICING MY EMERGENCY ESCAPE.
NOC
NOC
NOC
AND A VERY GOOD, ARTISTIC REPRESENTATION OF THIRD DYNASTY CRAFTSMANSHIP.
POP
OOPS!
OF COURSE, THIRD DYNASTY CRAFTSMANSHIP WASN'T VERY GOOD.
BUT NOW THAT THIS IS SOLVED, WE NEED TO DEAL WITH A MORE IMPORTANT PROBLEM...

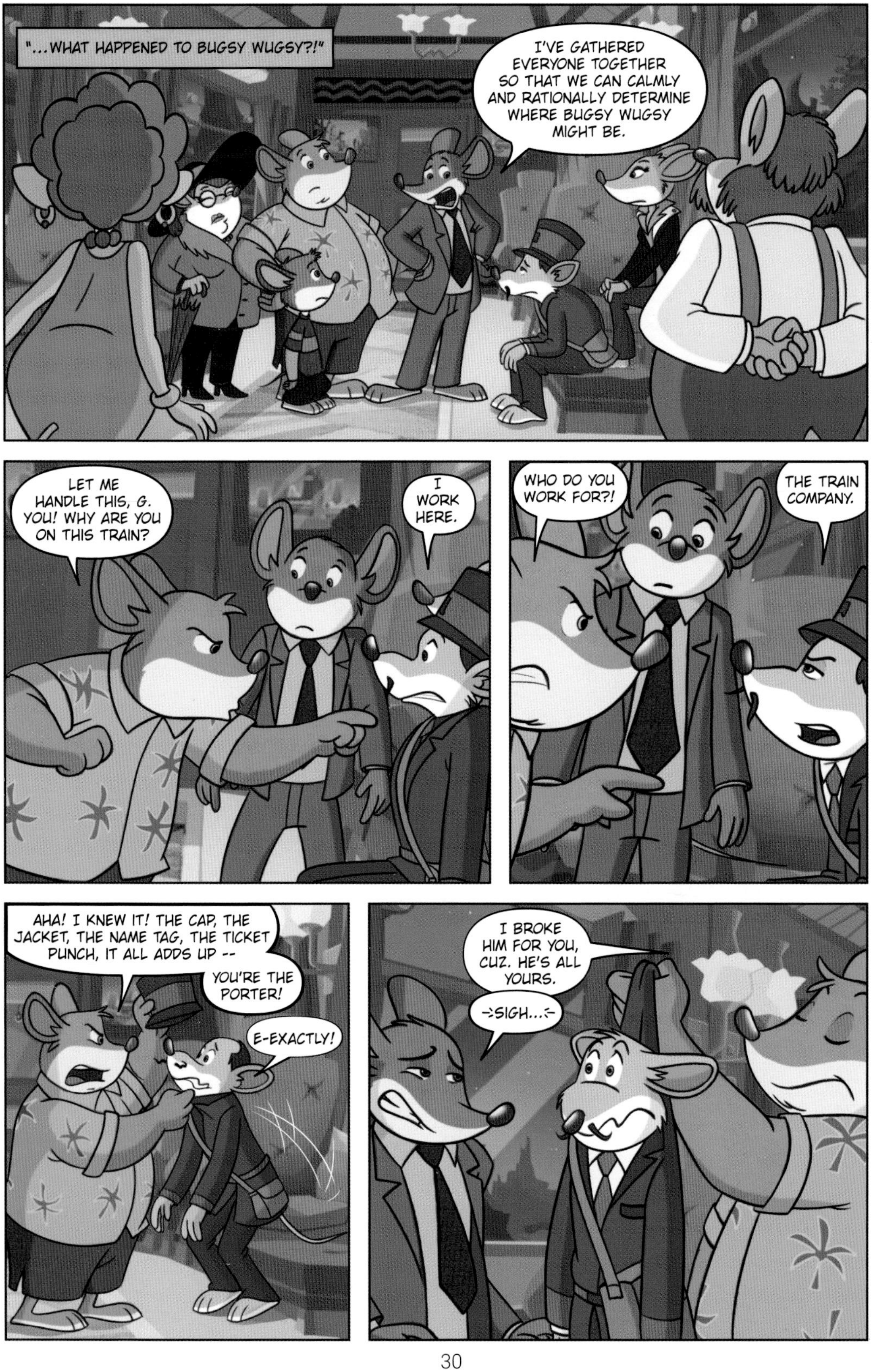
"...WHAT HAPPENED TO BUGSY WUGSY?!"
I'VE GATHERED EVERYONE TOGETHER SO THAT WE CAN CALMLY AND RATIONALLY DETERMINE WHERE BUGSY WUGSY MIGHT BE.
LET ME HANDLE THIS, G. YOU! WHY ARE YOU ON THIS TRAIN?
I WORK HERE.
WHO DO YOU WORK FOR?!
THE TRAIN COMPANY.
AHA! I KNEW IT! THE CAP, THE JACKET, THE NAME TAG, THE TICKET PUNCH, IT ALL ADDS UP --
YOU'RE THE PORTER!
E-EXACTLY!
I BROKE HIM FOR YOU, CUZ. HE'S ALL YOURS.
-SIGH...-

RIGHT. UM, LET'S GET BACK TO BUGSY WUGSY.

SINCE THE TRAIN HAS NEVER STOPPED, WE MUST ASSUME THAT SHE IS STILL ON BOARD AS WELL AS THE PERSON RESPONSIBLE FOR HER DISAPPEARANCE.

THE PORTER DID NOT DO IT!

BUT IT MUST BE HIM! HE THREATENED US!

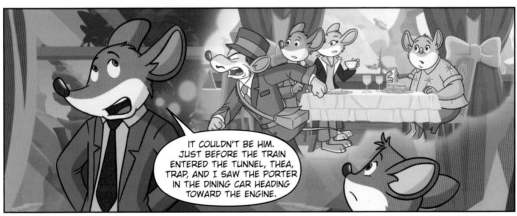

IT COULDN'T BE HIM. JUST BEFORE THE TRAIN ENTERED THE TUNNEL, THEA, TRAP, AND I SAW THE PORTER IN THE DINING CAR HEADING TOWARD THE ENGINE.

YEAH, YOU'RE RIGHT.

HE WAS NOWHERE NEAR BUGSY WUGSY WHEN SHE WENT MISSING.

FOR ALL THE MOZZARELLA! THEN IT MUST HAVE BEEN ONE OF US.

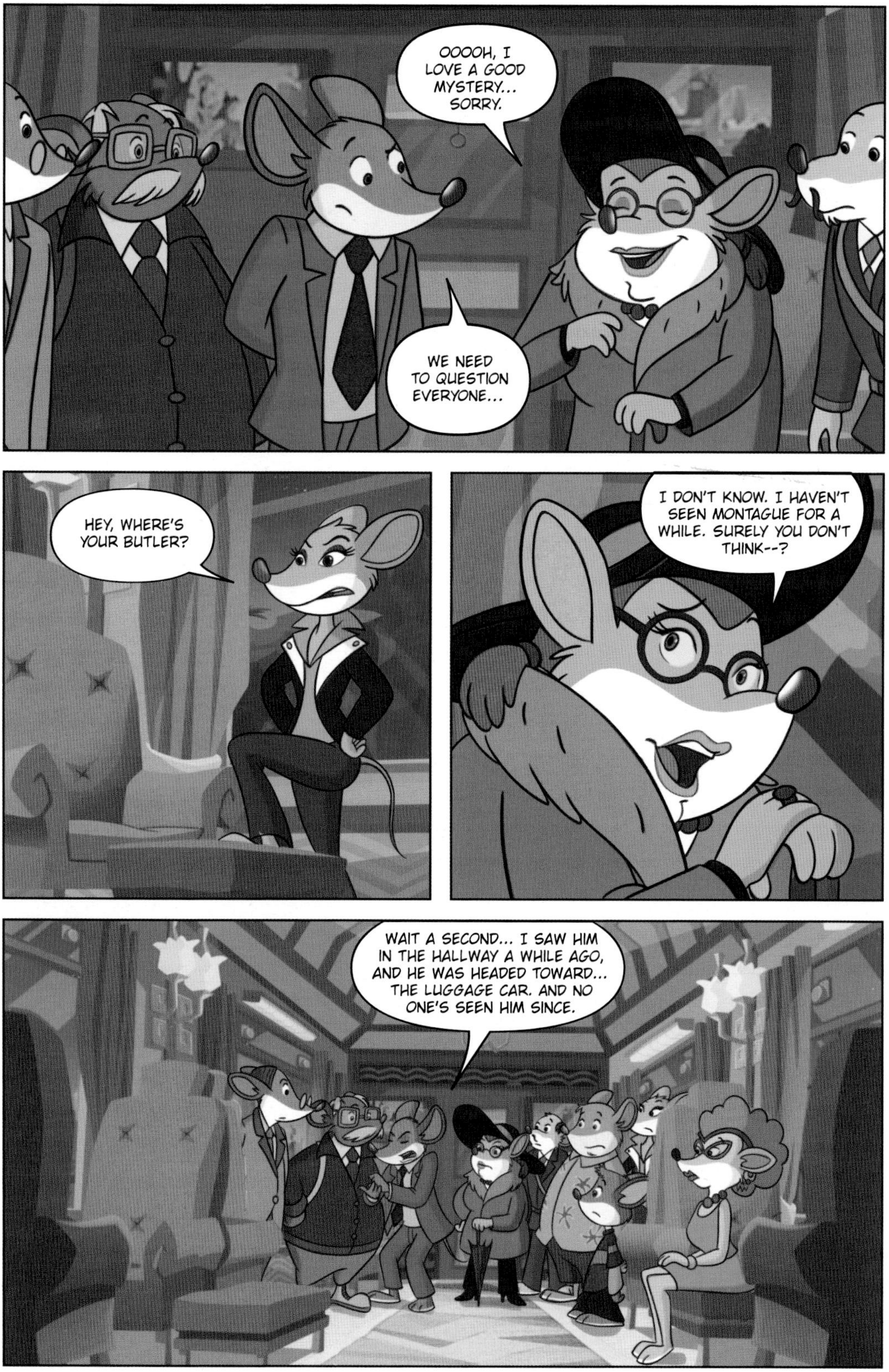
OOOOH, I LOVE A GOOD MYSTERY... SORRY.
WE NEED TO QUESTION EVERYONE...
HEY, WHERE'S YOUR BUTLER?
I DON'T KNOW. I HAVEN'T SEEN MONTAGUE FOR A WHILE. SURELY YOU DON'T THINK--?
WAIT A SECOND... I SAW HIM IN THE HALLWAY A WHILE AGO, AND HE WAS HEADED TOWARD... THE LUGGAGE CAR. AND NO ONE'S SEEN HIM SINCE.

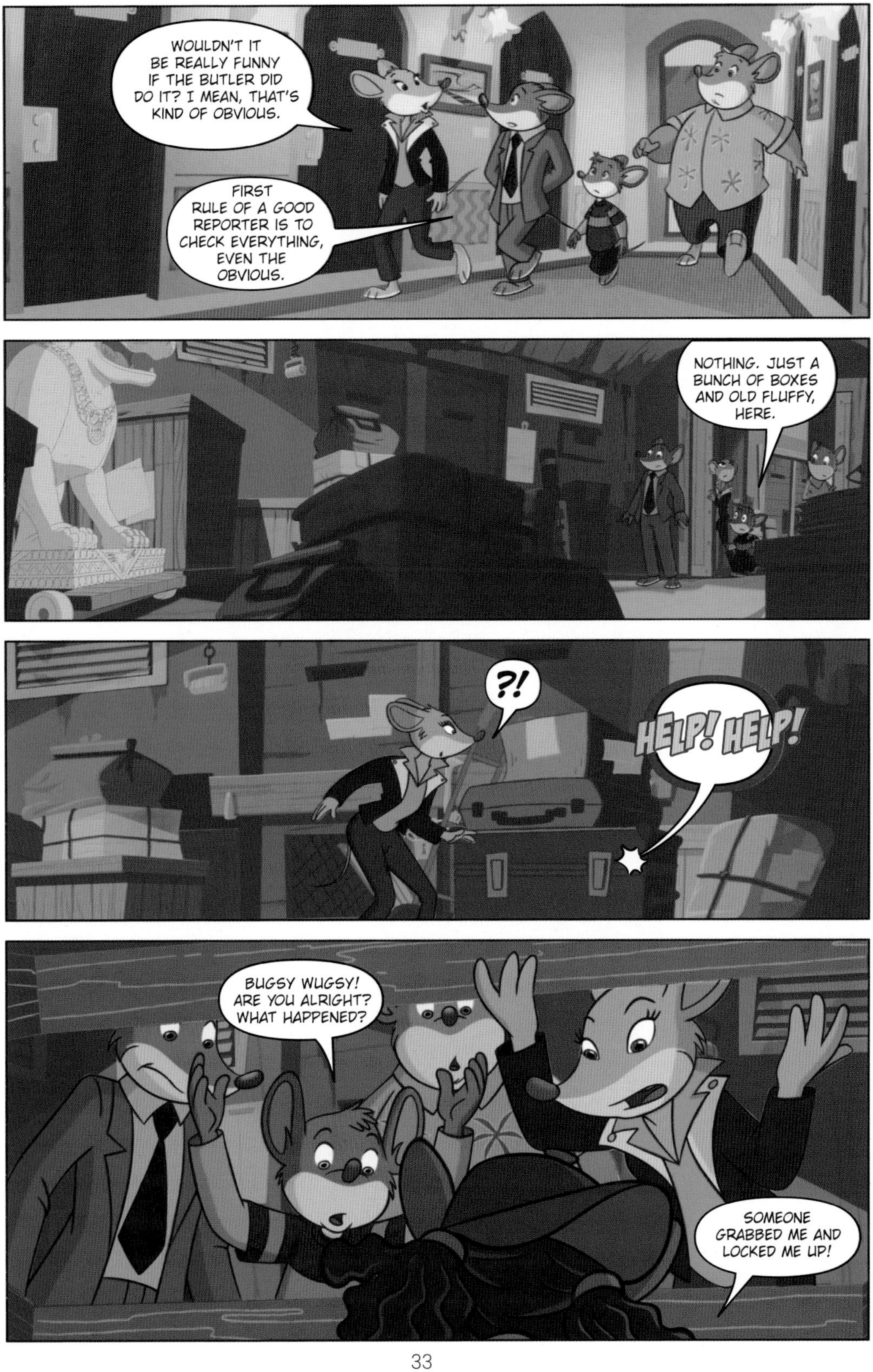
WOULDN'T IT BE REALLY FUNNY IF THE BUTLER DID DO IT? I MEAN, THAT'S KIND OF OBVIOUS.
FIRST RULE OF A GOOD REPORTER IS TO CHECK EVERYTHING, EVEN THE OBVIOUS.
NOTHING. JUST A BUNCH OF BOXES AND OLD FLUFFY, HERE.
?!
HELP! HELP!
BUGSY WUGSY! ARE YOU ALRIGHT? WHAT HAPPENED?
SOMEONE GRABBED ME AND LOCKED ME UP!

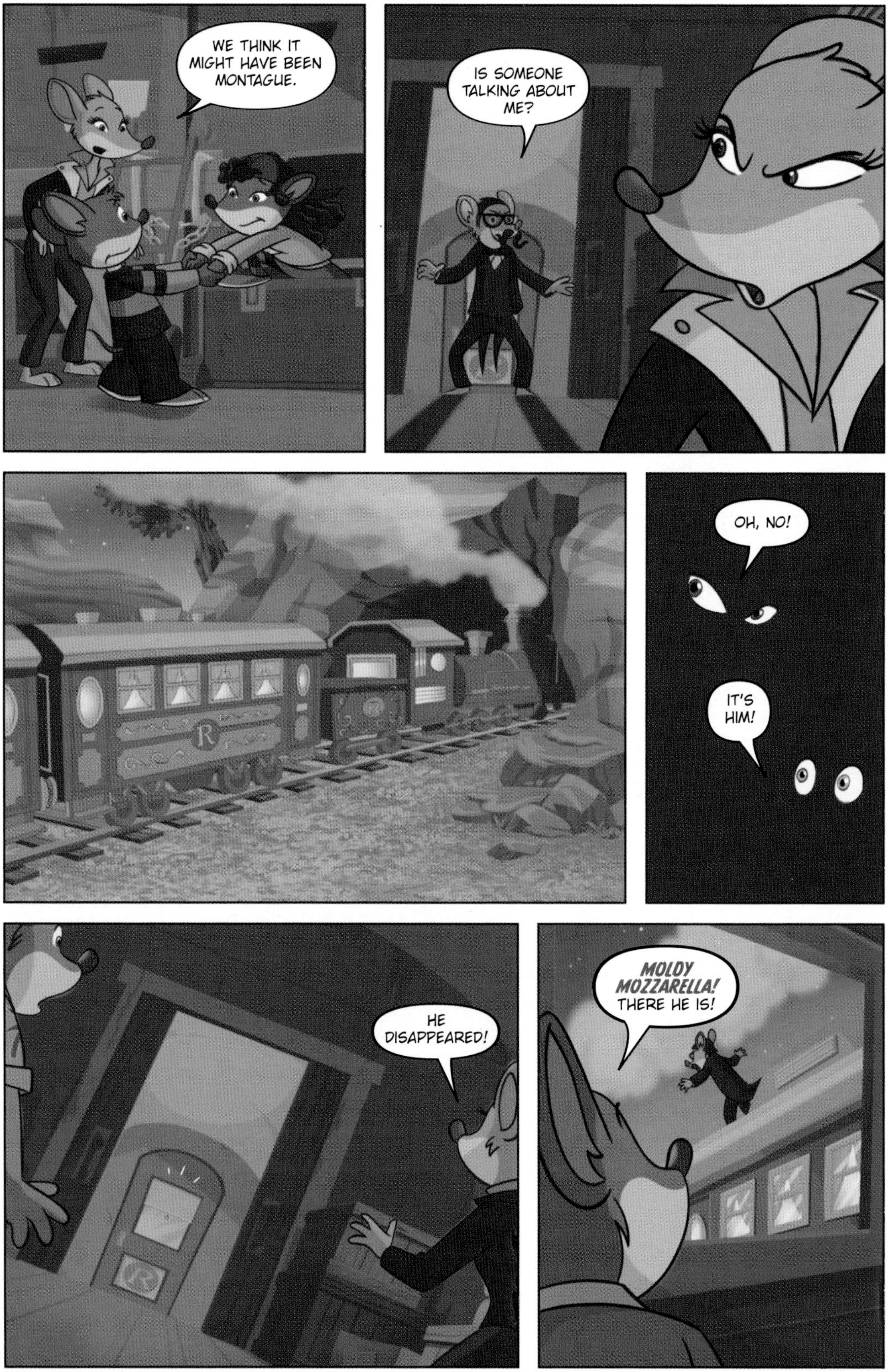
WE THINK IT MIGHT HAVE BEEN MONTAGUE.
IS SOMEONE TALKING ABOUT ME?
OH, NO!
IT'S HIM!
HE DISAPPEARED!
MOLDY MOZZARELLA! THERE HE IS!

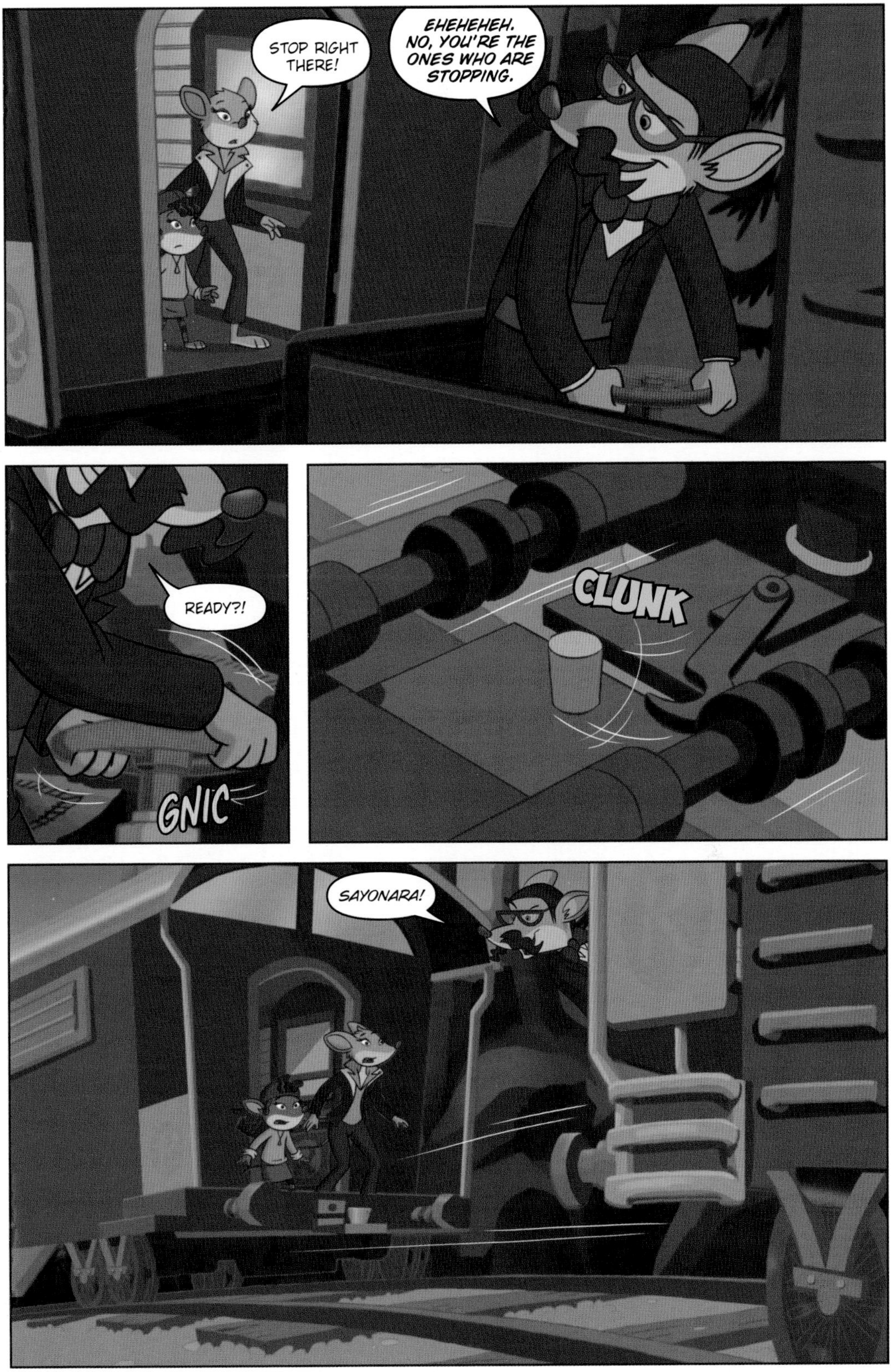
STOP RIGHT THERE!
EHEHEHEH. NO, YOU'RE THE ONES WHO ARE STOPPING.
READY?!
GNIC
CLUNK
SAYONARA!

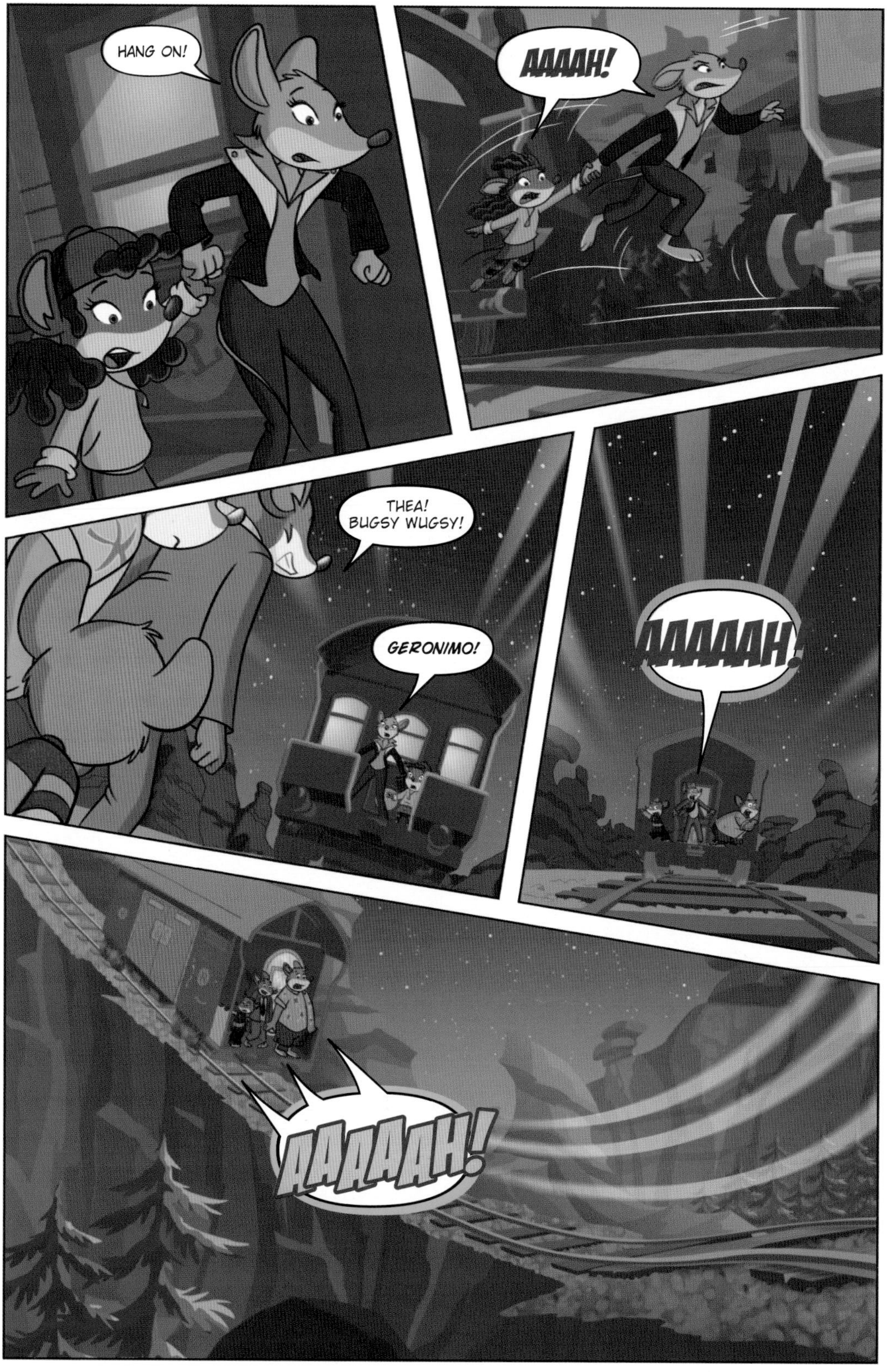
HANG ON!
AAAAH!
THEA! BUGSY WUGSY!
GERONIMO!
AAAAAH!
AAAAAH!

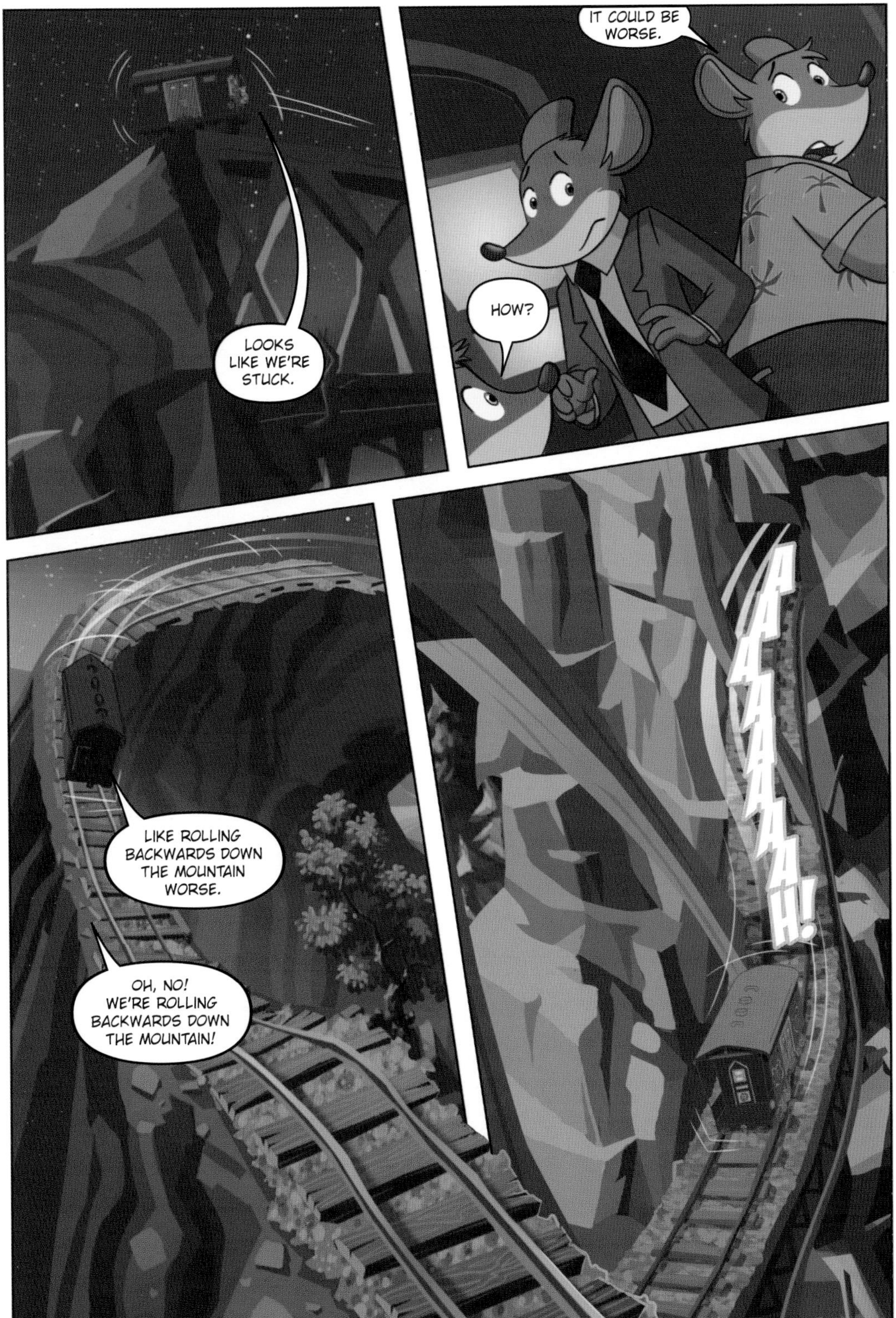
LOOKS LIKE WE'RE STUCK.
IT COULD BE WORSE.
HOW?
LIKE ROLLING BACKWARDS DOWN THE MOUNTAIN WORSE.
OH, NO! WE'RE ROLLING BACKWARDS DOWN THE MOUNTAIN!
AAAAAAAAH!

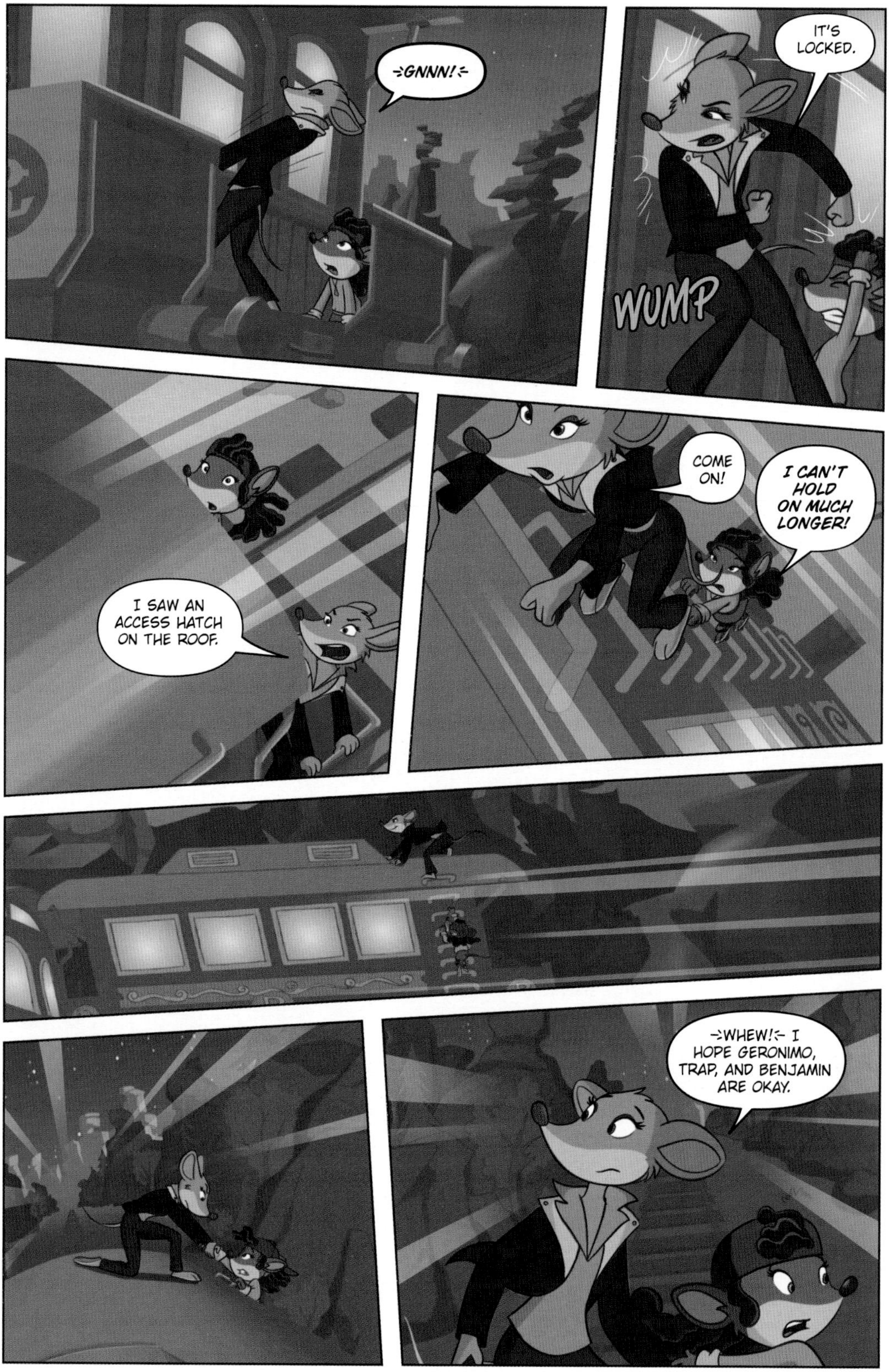

=GNNN!=
IT'S LOCKED.
WUMP
I SAW AN ACCESS HATCH ON THE ROOF.
COME ON!
I CAN'T HOLD ON MUCH LONGER!
=WHEW!= I HOPE GERONIMO, TRAP, AND BENJAMIN ARE OKAY.

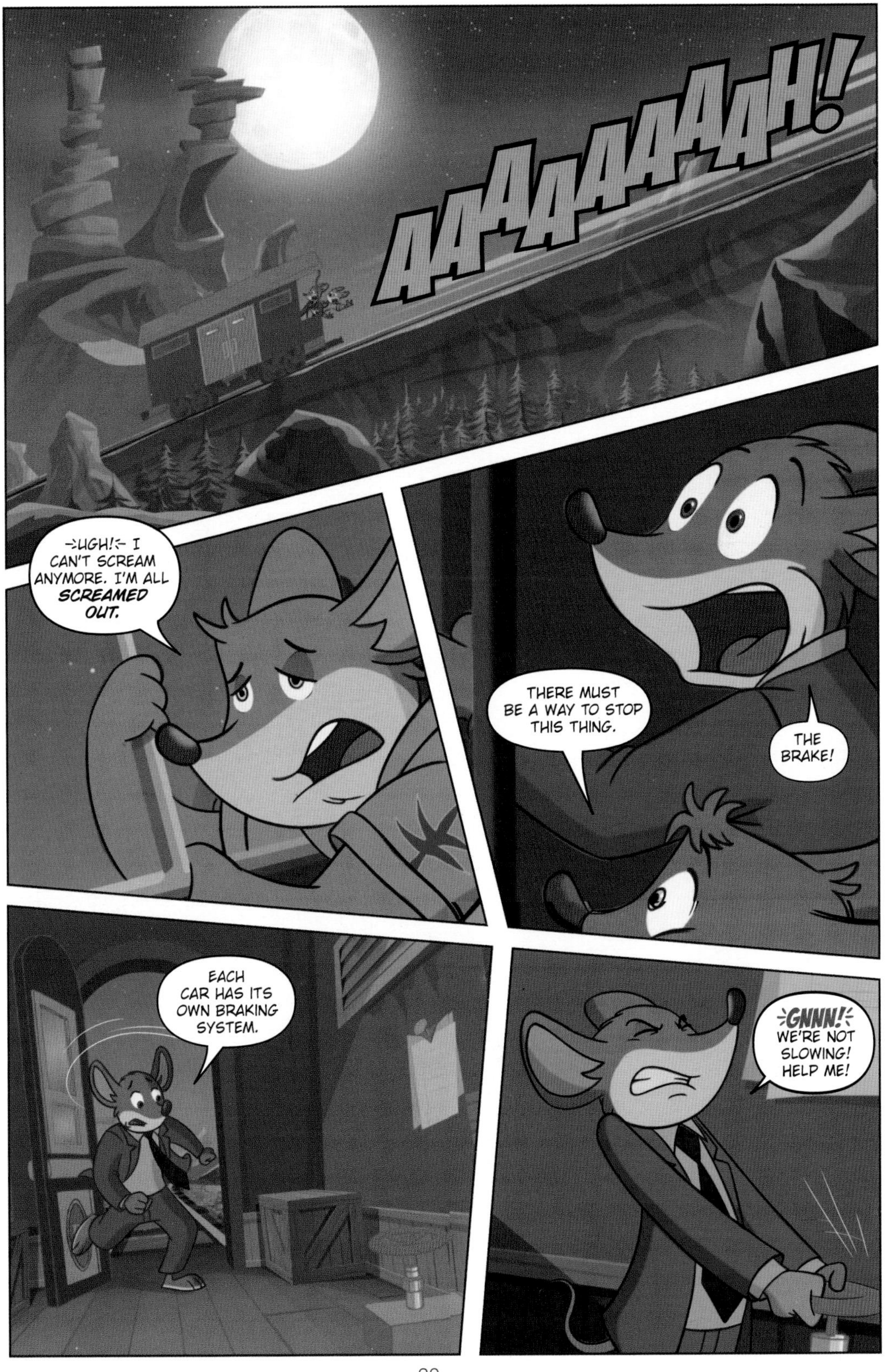
AAAAAAAAAH!
UGH! I CAN'T SCREAM ANYMORE. I'M ALL SCREAMED OUT.
THERE MUST BE A WAY TO STOP THIS THING.
THE BRAKE!
EACH CAR HAS ITS OWN BRAKING SYSTEM.
GNNN! WE'RE NOT SLOWING! HELP ME!

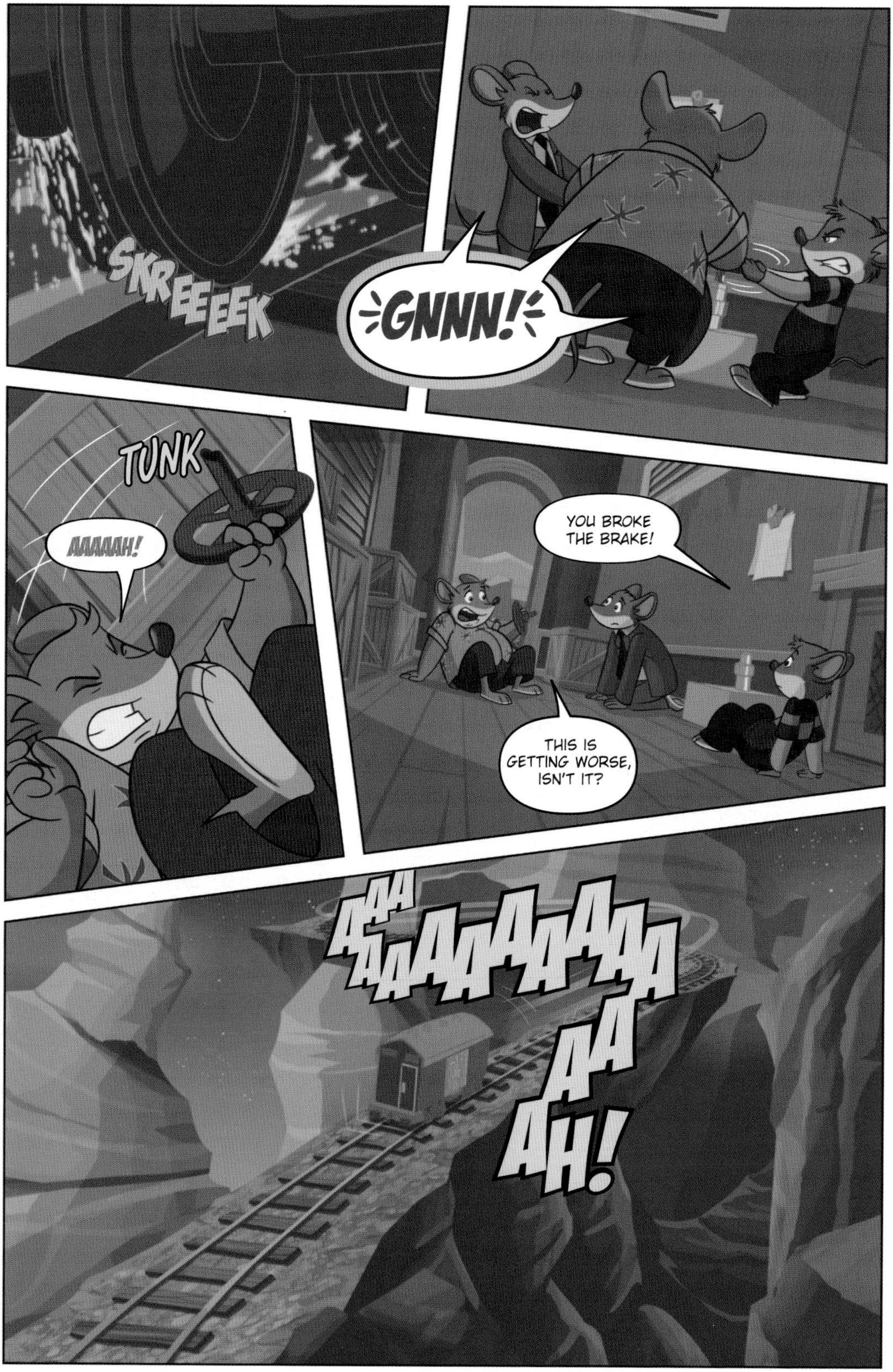
SKREEEEEK
GNNN!
TUNK
AAAAAAH!
YOU BROKE THE BRAKE!
THIS IS GETTING WORSE, ISN'T IT?
AAAAAAAAAAAAAAAAAAAAAH!

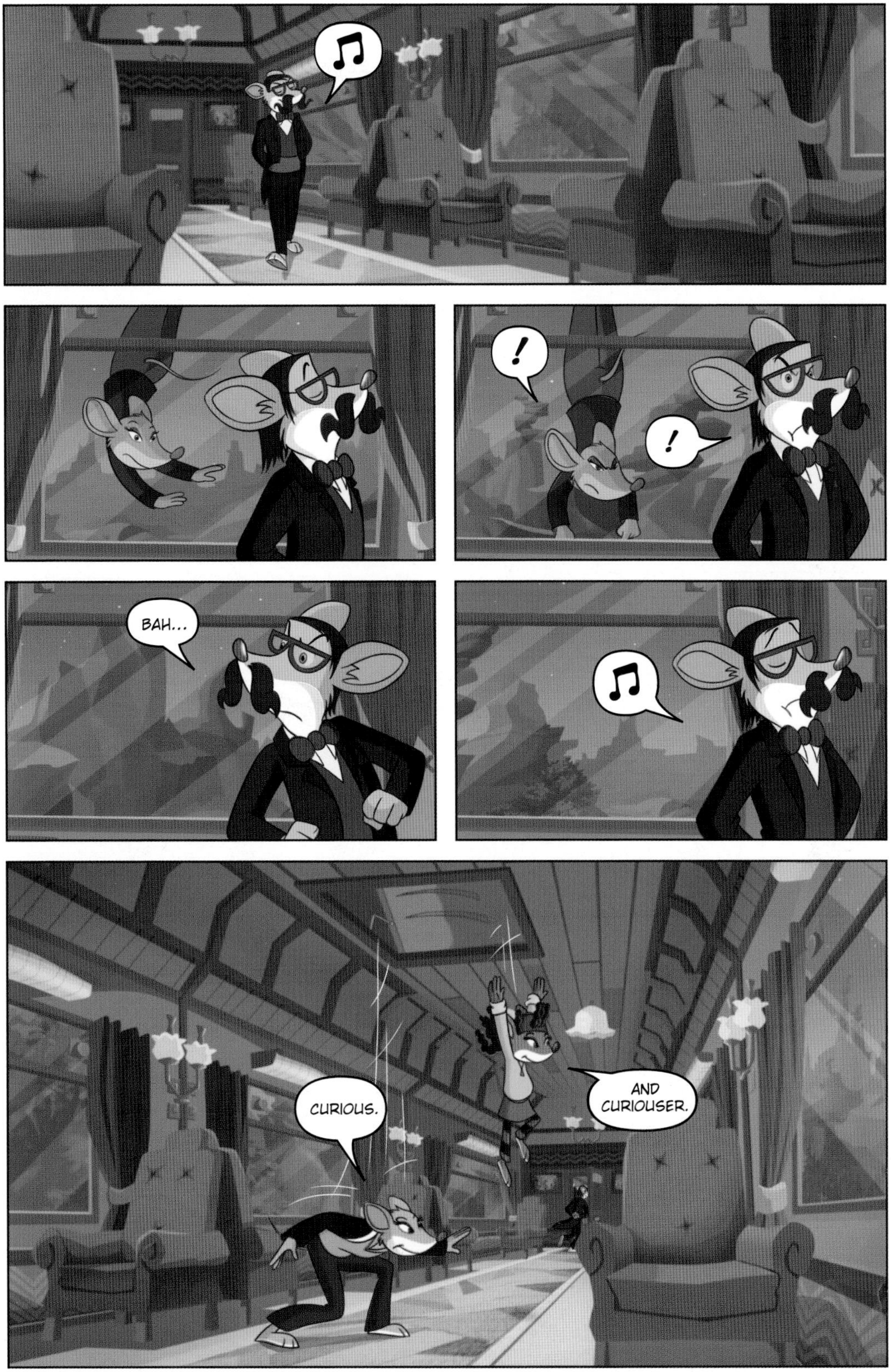
♫
!
!
BAH...
♫
CURIOUS.
AND CURIOUSER.

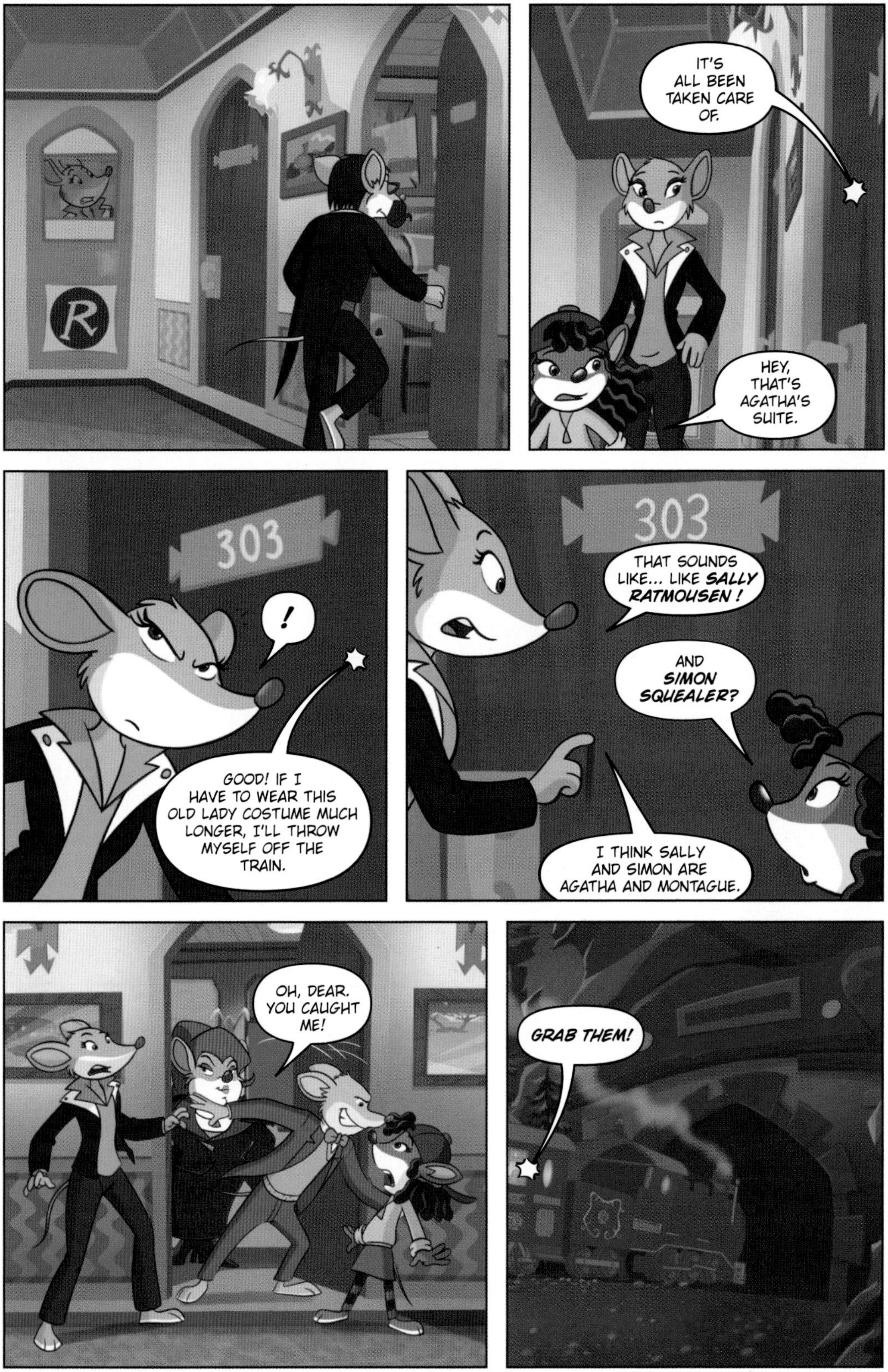
IT'S ALL BEEN TAKEN CARE OF.
HEY, THAT'S AGATHA'S SUITE.
303
!
GOOD! IF I HAVE TO WEAR THIS OLD LADY COSTUME MUCH LONGER, I'LL THROW MYSELF OFF THE TRAIN.
303
THAT SOUNDS LIKE... LIKE SALLY RATMOUSEN !
AND SIMON SQUEALER?
I THINK SALLY AND SIMON ARE AGATHA AND MONTAGUE.
OH, DEAR. YOU CAUGHT ME!
GRAB THEM!

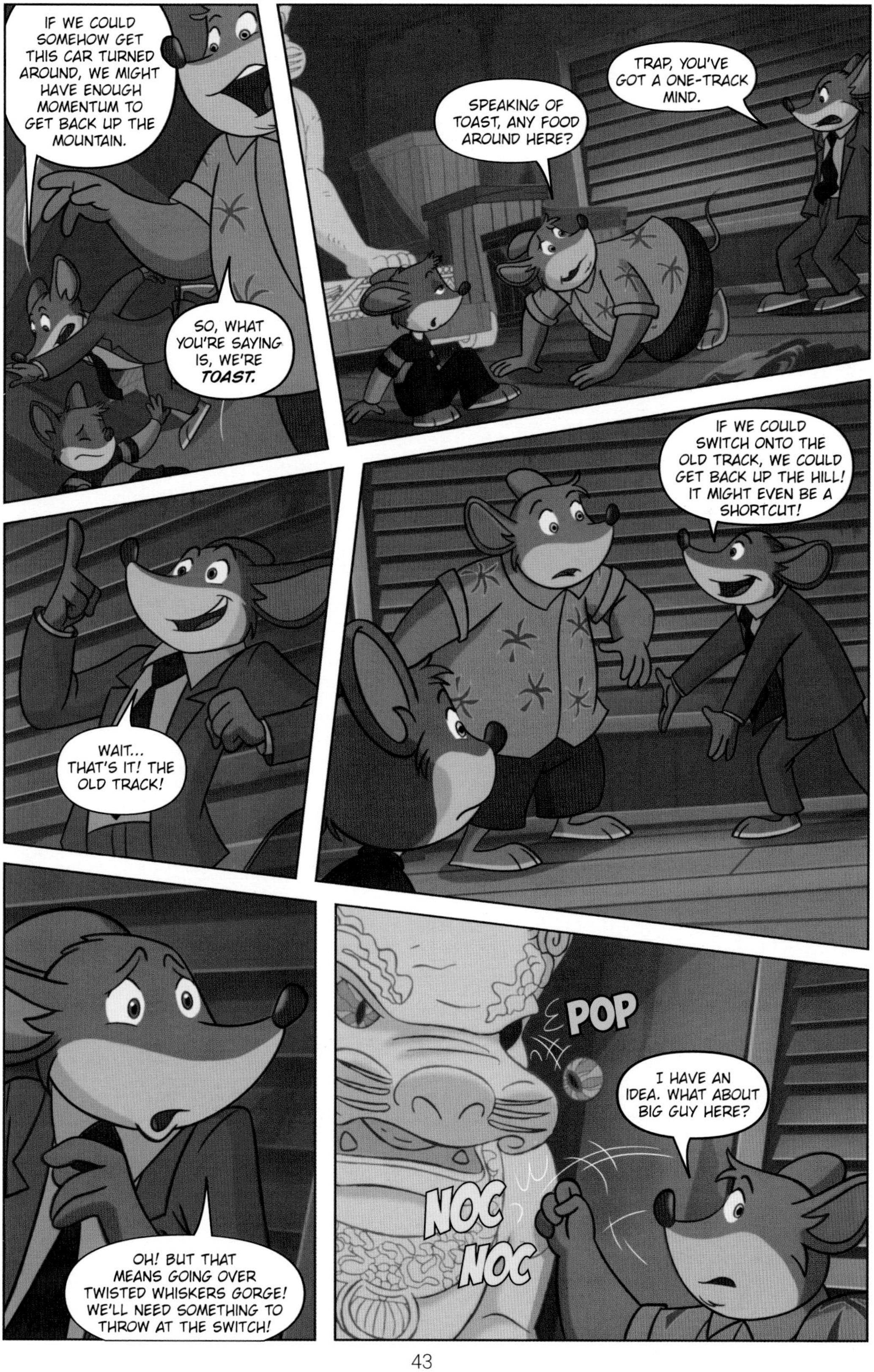
IF WE COULD SOMEHOW GET THIS CAR TURNED AROUND, WE MIGHT HAVE ENOUGH MOMENTUM TO GET BACK UP THE MOUNTAIN.
SO, WHAT YOU'RE SAYING IS, WE'RE TOAST.
SPEAKING OF TOAST, ANY FOOD AROUND HERE?
TRAP, YOU'VE GOT A ONE-TRACK MIND.
WAIT... THAT'S IT! THE OLD TRACK!
IF WE COULD SWITCH ONTO THE OLD TRACK, WE COULD GET BACK UP THE HILL! IT MIGHT EVEN BE A SHORTCUT!
OH! BUT THAT MEANS GOING OVER TWISTED WHISKERS GORGE! WE'LL NEED SOMETHING TO THROW AT THE SWITCH!
POP
NOC
NOC
I HAVE AN IDEA. WHAT ABOUT BIG GUY HERE?

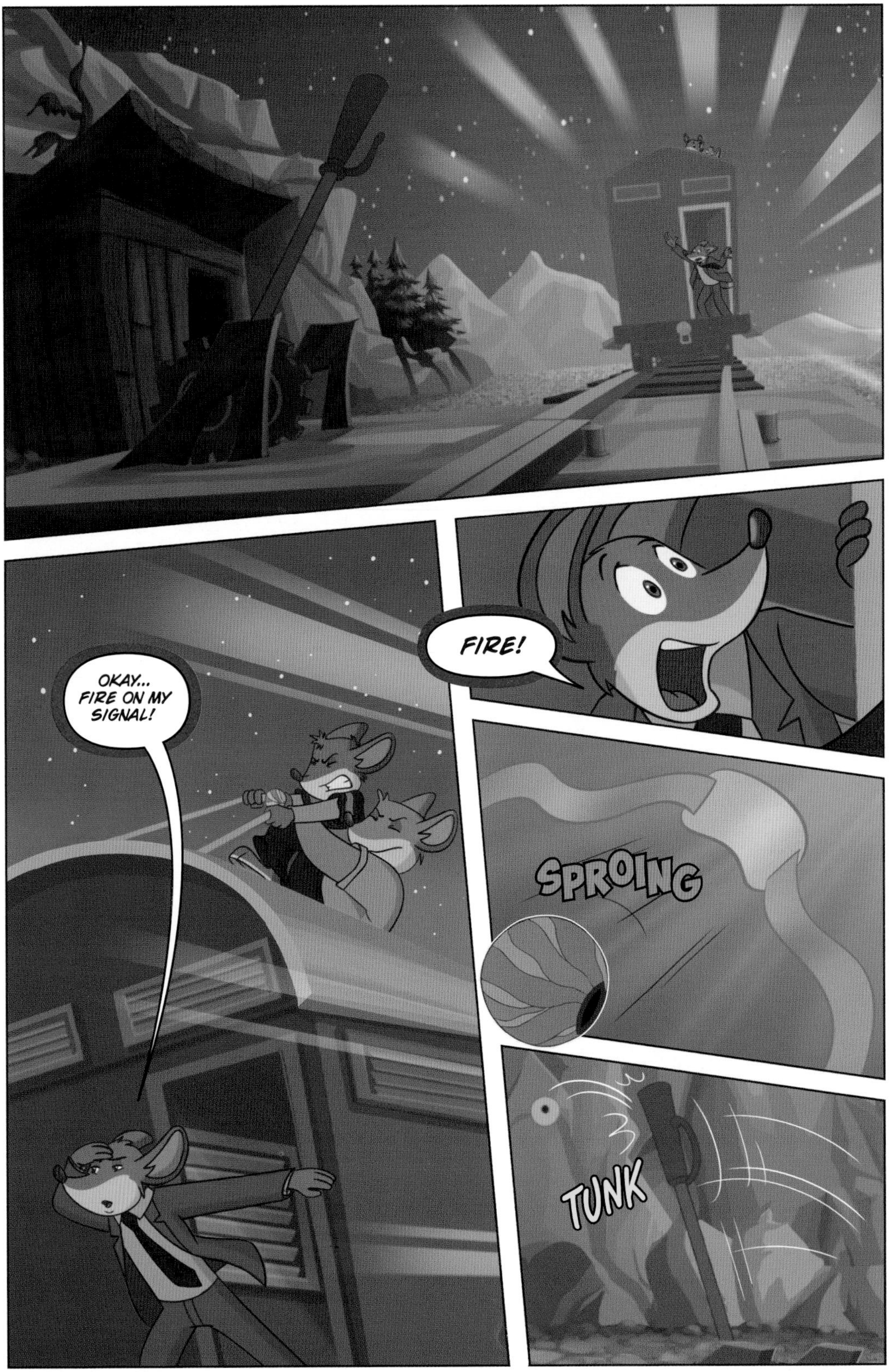

OKAY... FIRE ON MY SIGNAL!
FIRE!
SPROING
TUNK

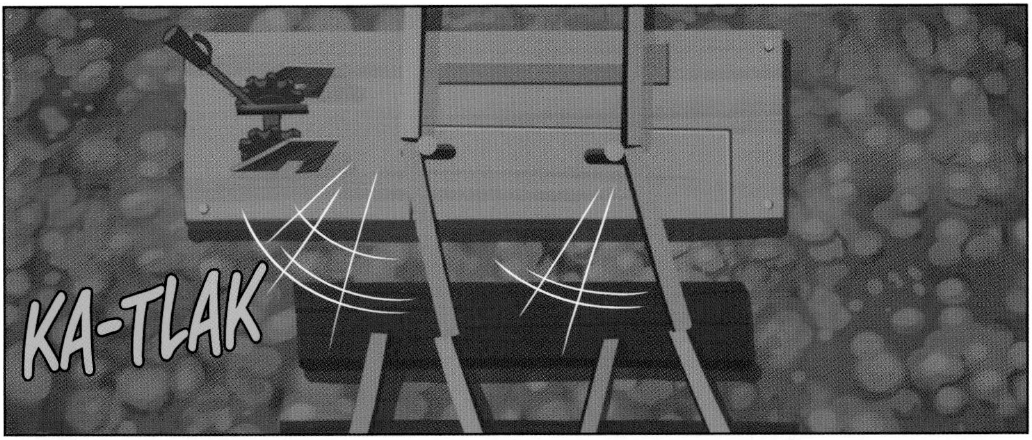
KA-TLAK

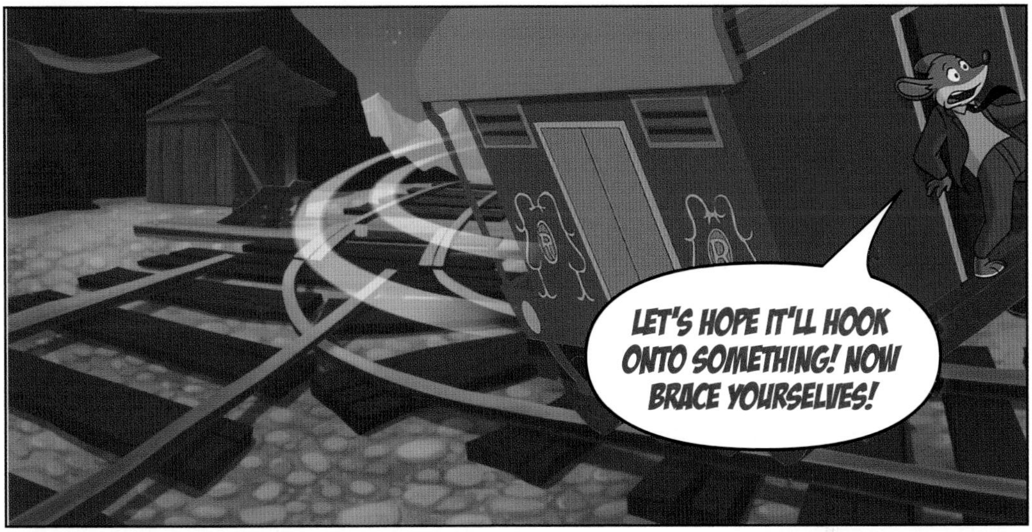
LET'S HOPE IT'LL HOOK ONTO SOMETHING! NOW BRACE YOURSELVES!

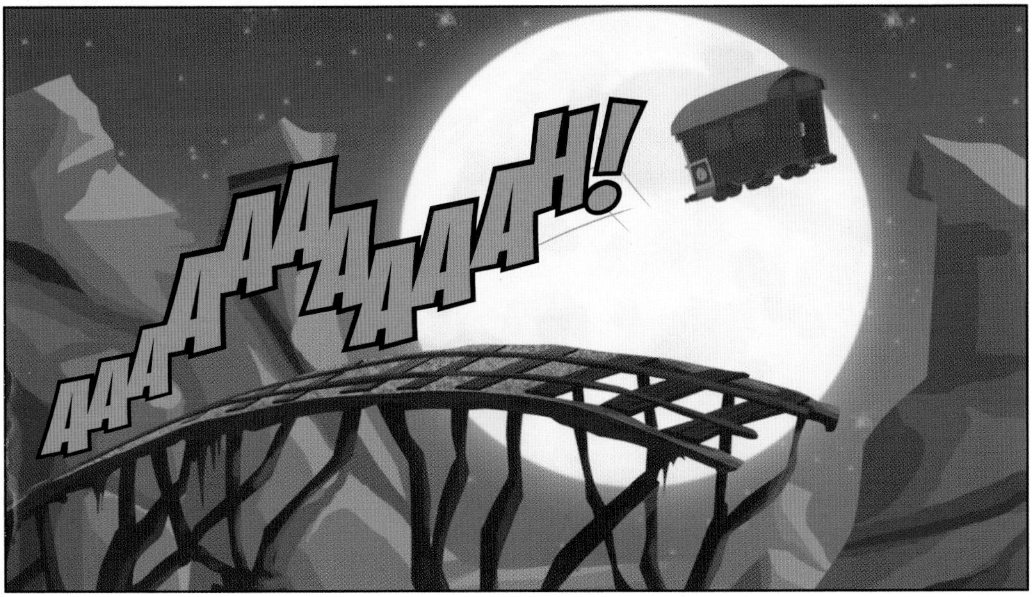
AAAAAAAAAAAAAH!

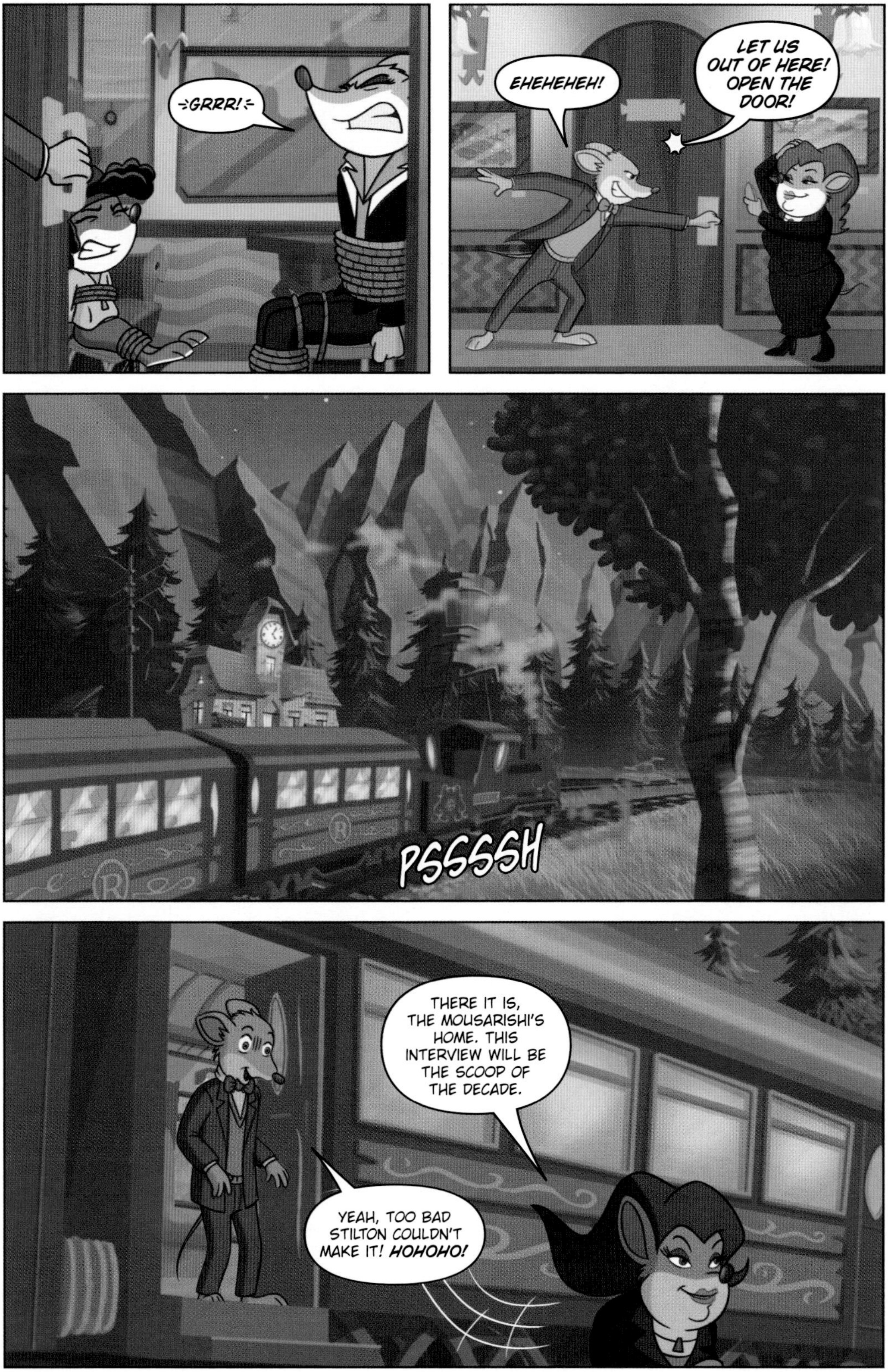

-GRRR!-
EHEHEHEH!
LET US OUT OF HERE! OPEN THE DOOR!
PSSSSH
THERE IT IS, THE MOUSARISHI'S HOME. THIS INTERVIEW WILL BE THE SCOOP OF THE DECADE.
YEAH, TOO BAD STILTON COULDN'T MAKE IT! HOHOHO!

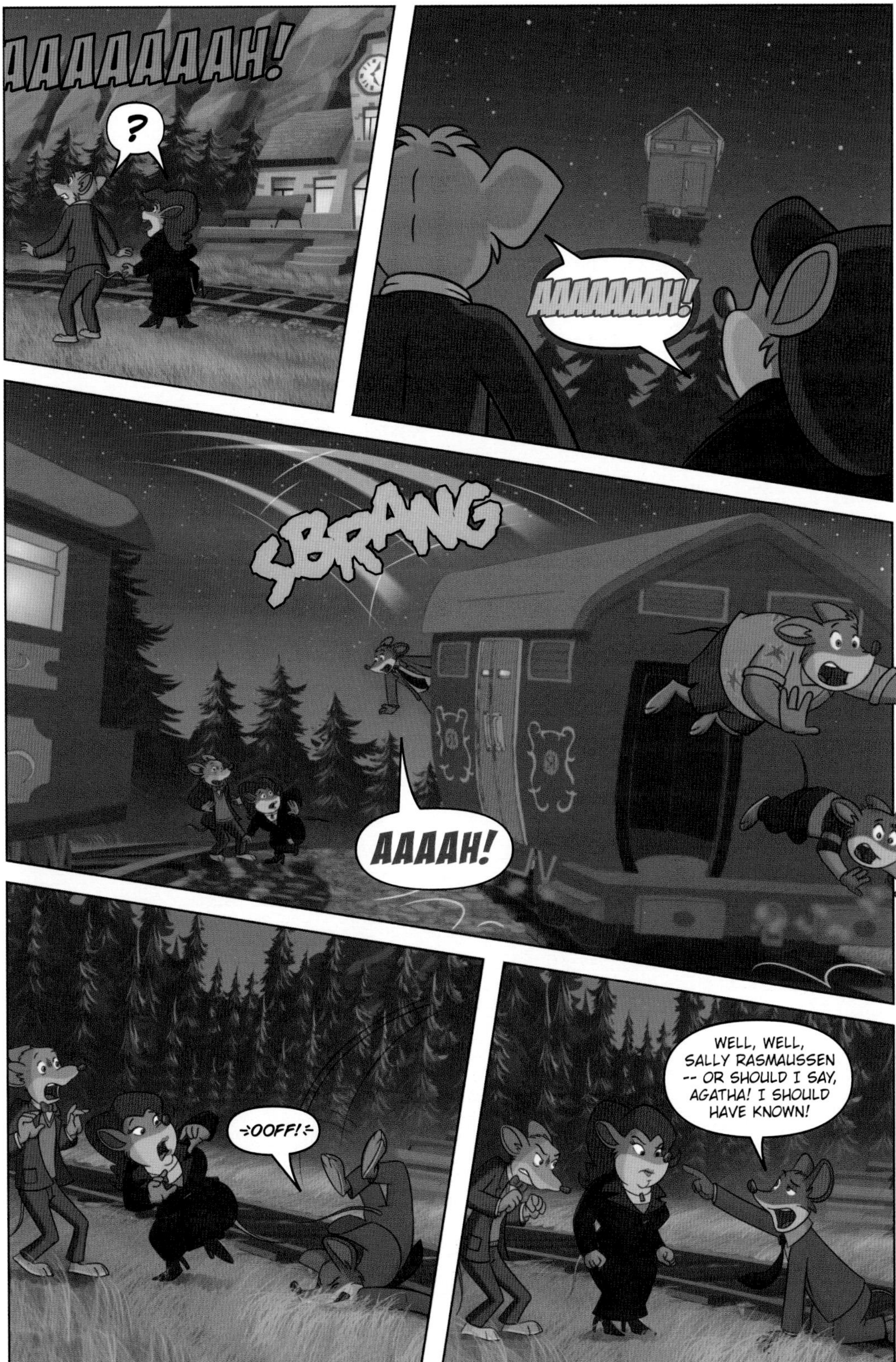
AAAAAAAH!
?
AAAAAAAH!
SBRANG
AAAAH!
OOFF!
WELL, WELL, SALLY RASMAUSSEN -- OR SHOULD I SAY, AGATHA! I SHOULD HAVE KNOWN!

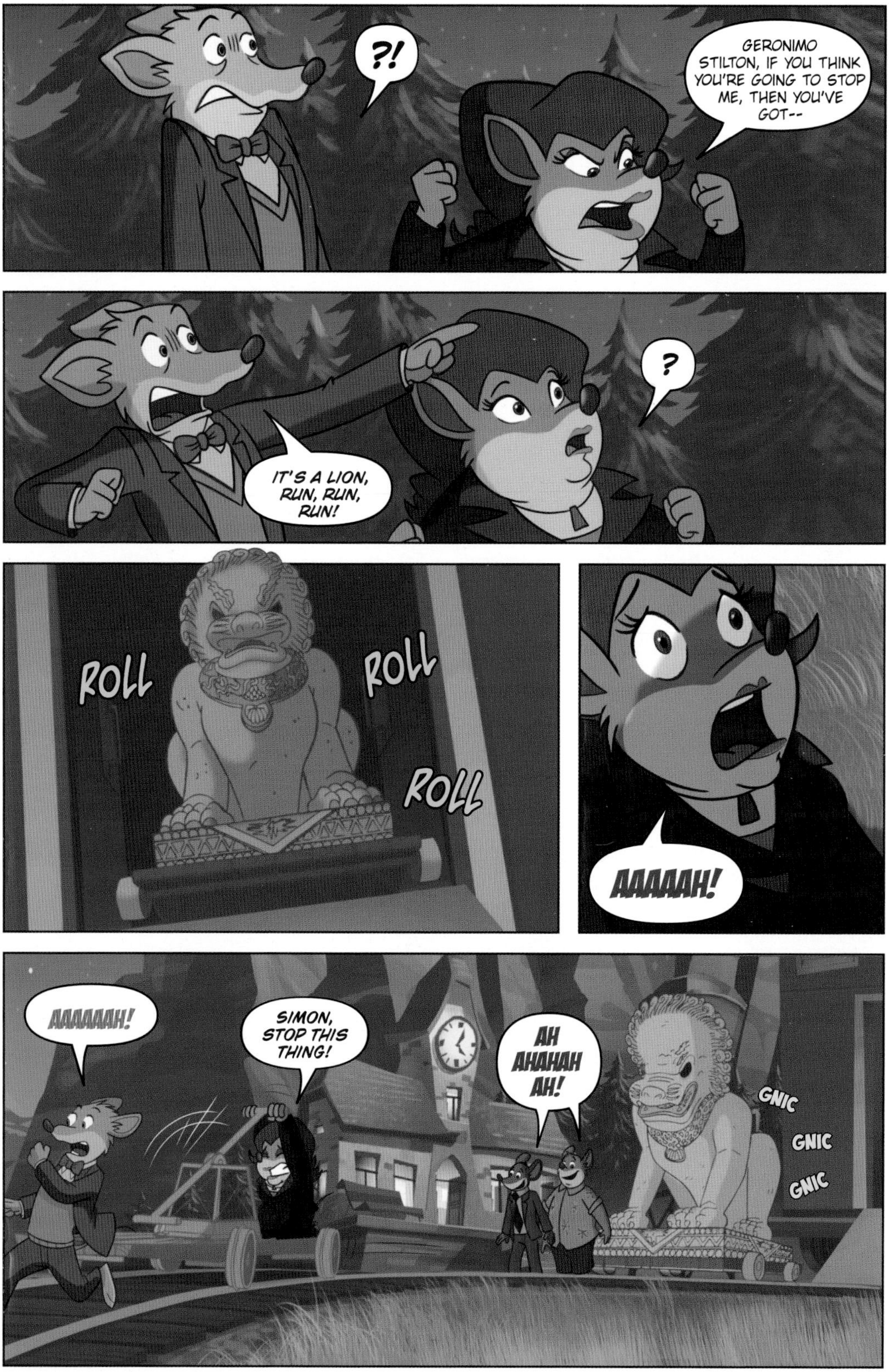

?!
GERONIMO STILTON, IF YOU THINK YOU'RE GOING TO STOP ME, THEN YOU'VE GOT--
IT'S A LION, RUN, RUN, RUN!
?
ROLL
ROLL
ROLL
AAAAAH!
AAAAAAH!
SIMON, STOP THIS THING!
AH AHAHAH AH!
GNIC
GNIC
GNIC

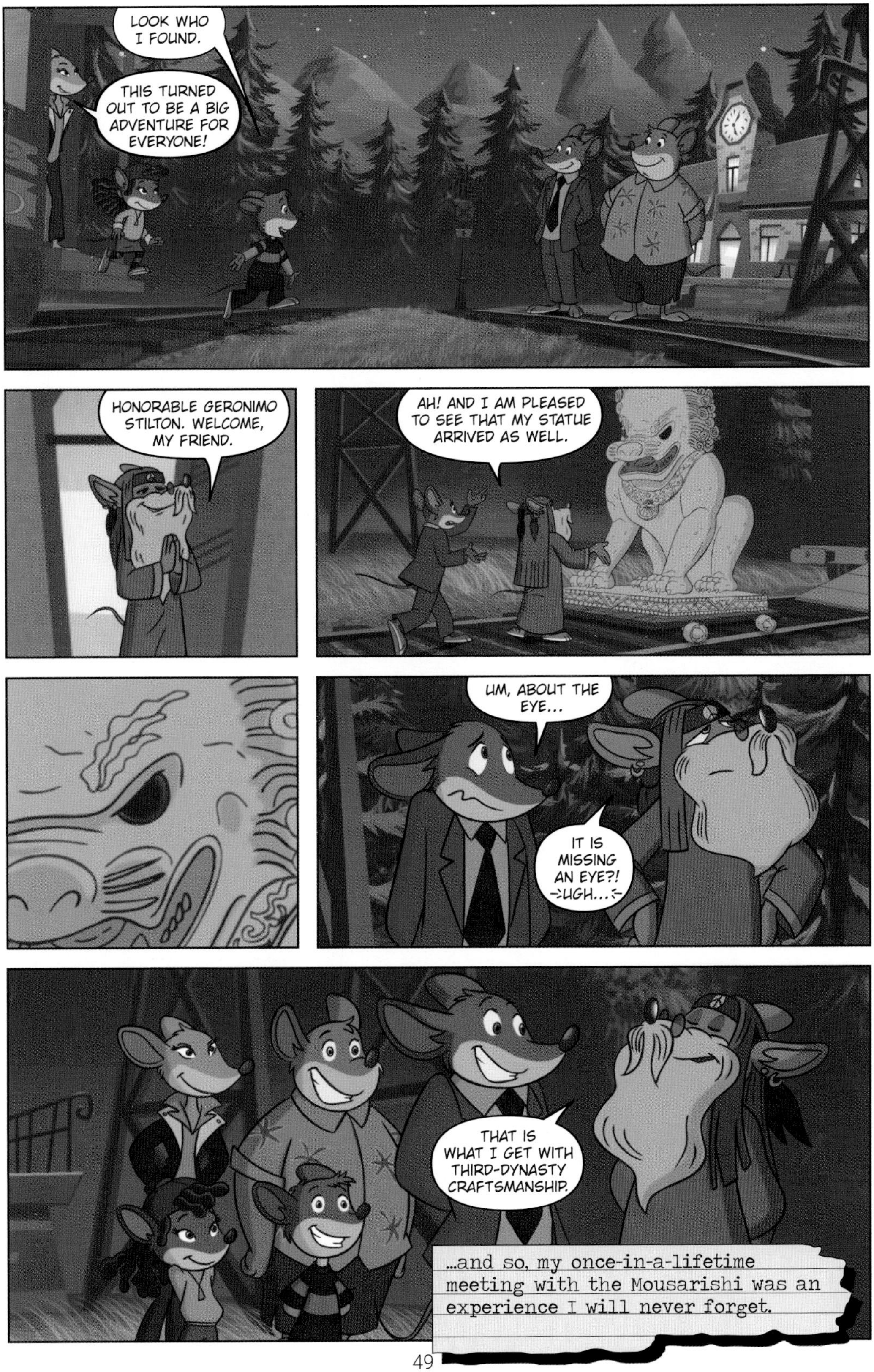
LOOK WHO I FOUND.
THIS TURNED OUT TO BE A BIG ADVENTURE FOR EVERYONE!
HONORABLE GERONIMO STILTON. WELCOME, MY FRIEND.
AH! AND I AM PLEASED TO SEE THAT MY STATUE ARRIVED AS WELL.
UM, ABOUT THE EYE...
IT IS MISSING AN EYE?! UGH...
THAT IS WHAT I GET WITH THIRD-DYNASTY CRAFTSMANSHIP.
...and so, my once-in-a-lifetime meeting with the Mousarishi was an experience I will never forget.

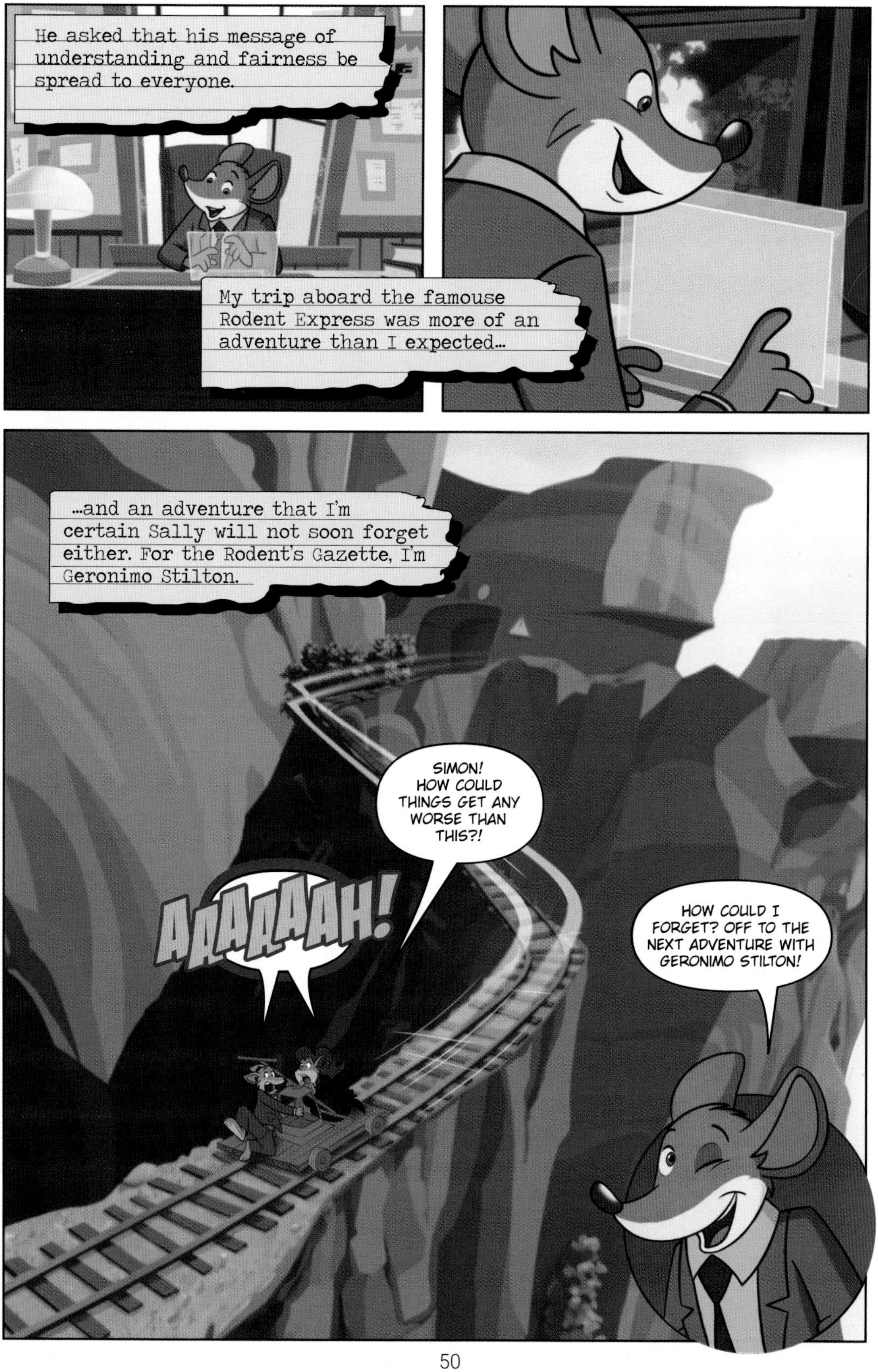
He asked that his message of understanding and fairness be spread to everyone.
My trip aboard the famouse Rodent Express was more of an adventure than I expected...
...and an adventure that I'm certain Sally will not soon forget either. For the Rodent's Gazette, I'm Geronimo Stilton.
AAAAAAH!
SIMON! HOW COULD THINGS GET ANY WORSE THAN THIS?!
HOW COULD I FORGET? OFF TO THE NEXT ADVENTURE WITH GERONIMO STILTON!

Watch Out For PAPERCUTZ™

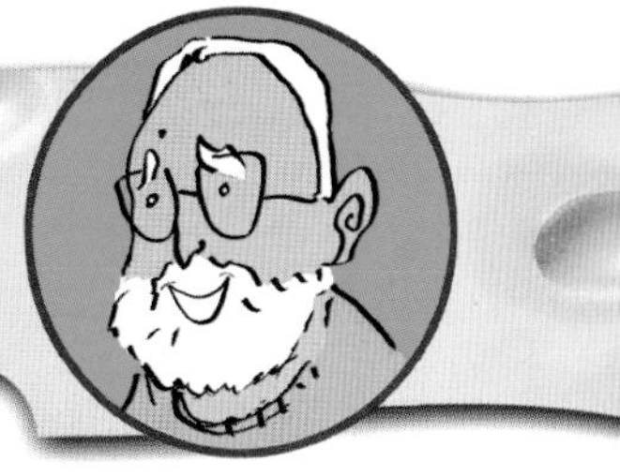

Welcome to the electrifying eleventh GERONIMO STILTON REPORTER graphic novel, "Mystery on the Rodent Express," the official comics adaptation of the eleventh episode of Geronimo Stilton Season One, written by Earl Kress, brought to you by Papercutz—those subway straphangers dedicated to publishing great graphic novels for all ages. I'm Salicrup, *Jim Salicrup*, the Editor-in-Chief and Man of Mystery, here to help uncover a few more mysteries…But first a *SPOILER WARNING*. If you haven't already read all of "Mystery on the Rodent Express," please don't read any further, as it will spoil some of the story's surprises. So, if you have read all of "Mystery on the Rodent Express," you may proceed…

If the character Agatha Moustie seemed familiar to you, and we're not talking about her secretly being Sally Ratmousen, Geronimo's unethical counterpart at *The Daily Rat*, it's because she's inspired by the real-life mystery author, Agatha Christie.

Dame Agatha Christie, was born September 15, 1890, and she died January 12, 1976. She was a world-famous English writer, best known for her 66 detective novels and 14 short story collections. (Gee, she was almost as prolific as Geronimo!) Her two most popular characters were the fictional detectives Miss Marple and Hercule Poirot. In 1971, she was made a Dame (DBE; Dame is an honorific title. The title of dame as the official equivalent of knight was introduced in 1917 with the introduction of the Order of the British Empire and was subsequently extended to the Royal Victorian Order in 1936.) for her contributions to literature. *Guinness World Records* lists Christie as the best-selling fiction writer of all time, her novels having sold more than two billion copies.

Famous real-life people are often used as inspiration for fictional characters. Sometimes the fictional character makes gentle fun of the real-life person, and that's called either a spoof or a parody. Other times fictional versions of real-life characters are used in *roman à clef* novels, which are thinly disguised stories about real events and people, where all the names have been changed to make it seem "fictional." In "Mystery on the Rodent Express," the character Agatha Moustie is more of a light-hearted *homage*—a show of respect to someone, sometimes by simple declaration but often by some more oblique reference, artistic or poetic.

Indeed, other elements of the story are also spoofy *homages* to elements of Agatha Christie's work. The title "Mystery on the Rodent Express" is clearly inspired by the title of her book, "Murder on the Orient Express," which has been adapted as a movie several times. When Geronimo gathers the passengers and the porter together to see if anyone can help him find Bugsy Wugsy, this is something that not only Agatha Christie's detectives would do, but something many detectives have done in mystery stories countless times. When Trap acts tough and bombards the porter with questions (only to discover that he's the porter!), he's parodying the tough cop or detective that tries to get information from a possible suspect or witness. After everyone realizes that Montague isn't among the passengers gathered together by Geronimo, Thea asks, "Wouldn't it be really funny if the butler did it?" That's because in so many Agatha Christie-style mysteries, butlers are often suspects and sometimes the bad guy, that it became a joke to conclude, "the butler did it!"

This isn't the first time Agatha Christie has inspired a GERONIMO STILTON story. If the name of one of her famous detectives seemed familiar, it may be because it sounded a lot like the name of the famouse detective Hercule Poirat. He's the clever, banana-loving detective who runs the Squeak Agency and is a longtime friend of Geronimo—they went to preschool together! While Hercule has appeared in many GERONIMO STILTON chapter books published by our friends at Scholastic, he's only appeared in one GERONIMO STILTON graphic novel published by Papercutz—GERONIMO STILTON #3 "The Coliseum Con," which can also be found in GERONIMO STILTON 3 IN 1 #1.

While you might suspect that Geronimo Stilton must be a big fan of Agatha Moustie, we're not too sure if he'd like the title of Agatha Christie's long-running play (it holds the world record for longest initial run)—The Mousetrap.

Now that we've revealed the answers to mysteries that were so mysterious you probably didn't even know they existed, let there be no mystery as to what's coming your way in the next GERONIMO STILTON REPORTER graphic novel. It's a story entitled "The Mouse House of the Future" and you can check out a short preview on the very next page. So, until we meet again…

Thanks (for picking up this GERONIMO STILTON REPORTER graphic novel),

JIM

STAY IN TOUCH!

EMAIL:	salicrup@papercutz.com
WEB:	papercutz.com
TWITTER:	@papercutzgn
INSTAGRAM:	@papercutzgn
FACEBOOK:	PAPERCUTZGRAPHICNOVELS
SNAIL MAIL:	Papercutz, 160 Broadway, Suite 700, East Wing, New York, NY 10038

Go to papercutz.com and sign up for the free Papercutz e-newsletter!

Special Preview of GERONIMO STILTON REPORTER Graphic Novel #12 "The Mouse House of the Future"!

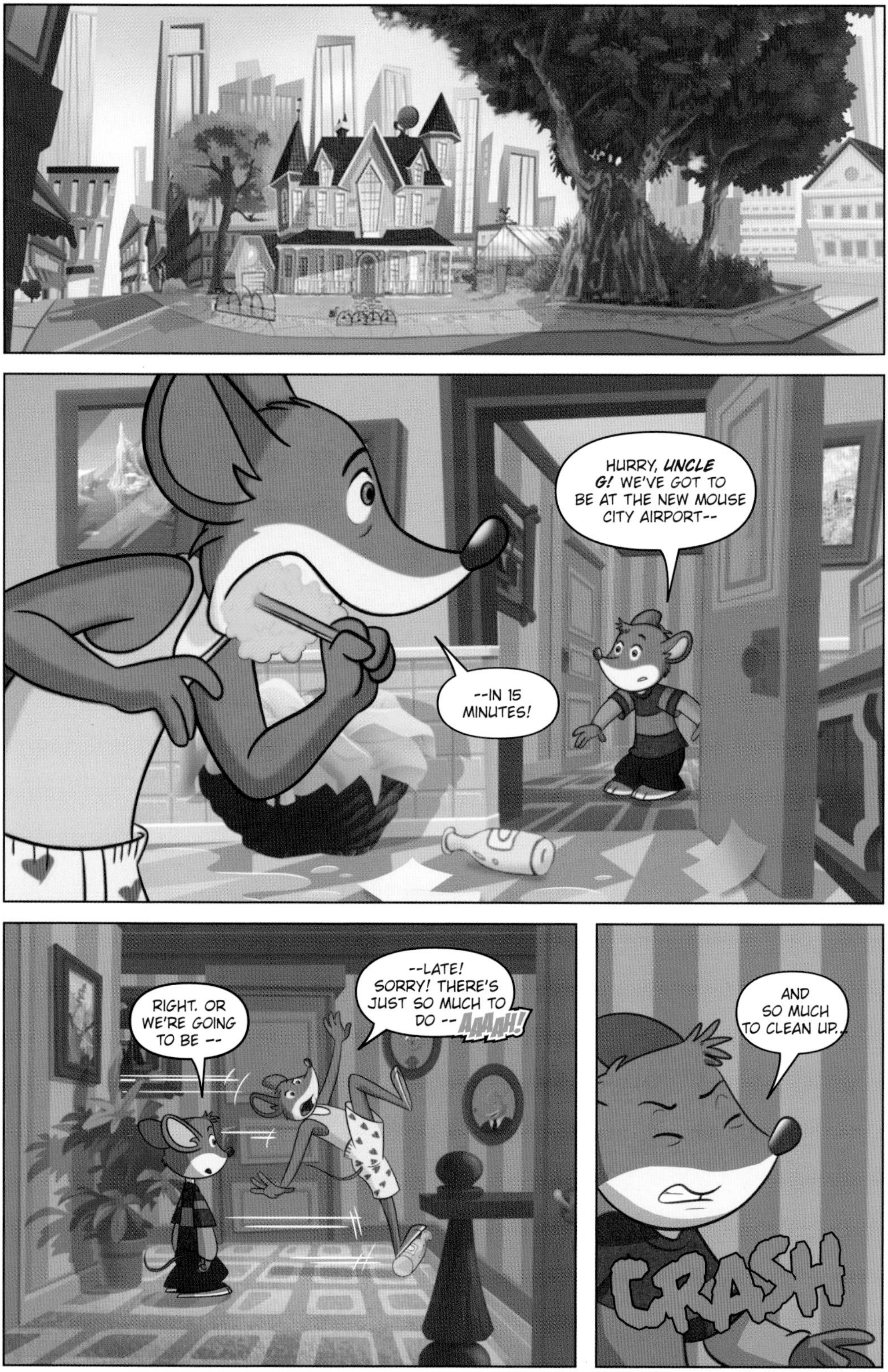
HURRY, *UNCLE G!* WE'VE GOT TO BE AT THE NEW MOUSE CITY AIRPORT--
--IN 15 MINUTES!
RIGHT. OR WE'RE GOING TO BE --
--LATE! SORRY! THERE'S JUST SO MUCH TO DO -- AAAAH!
AND SO MUCH TO CLEAN UP...
CRASH

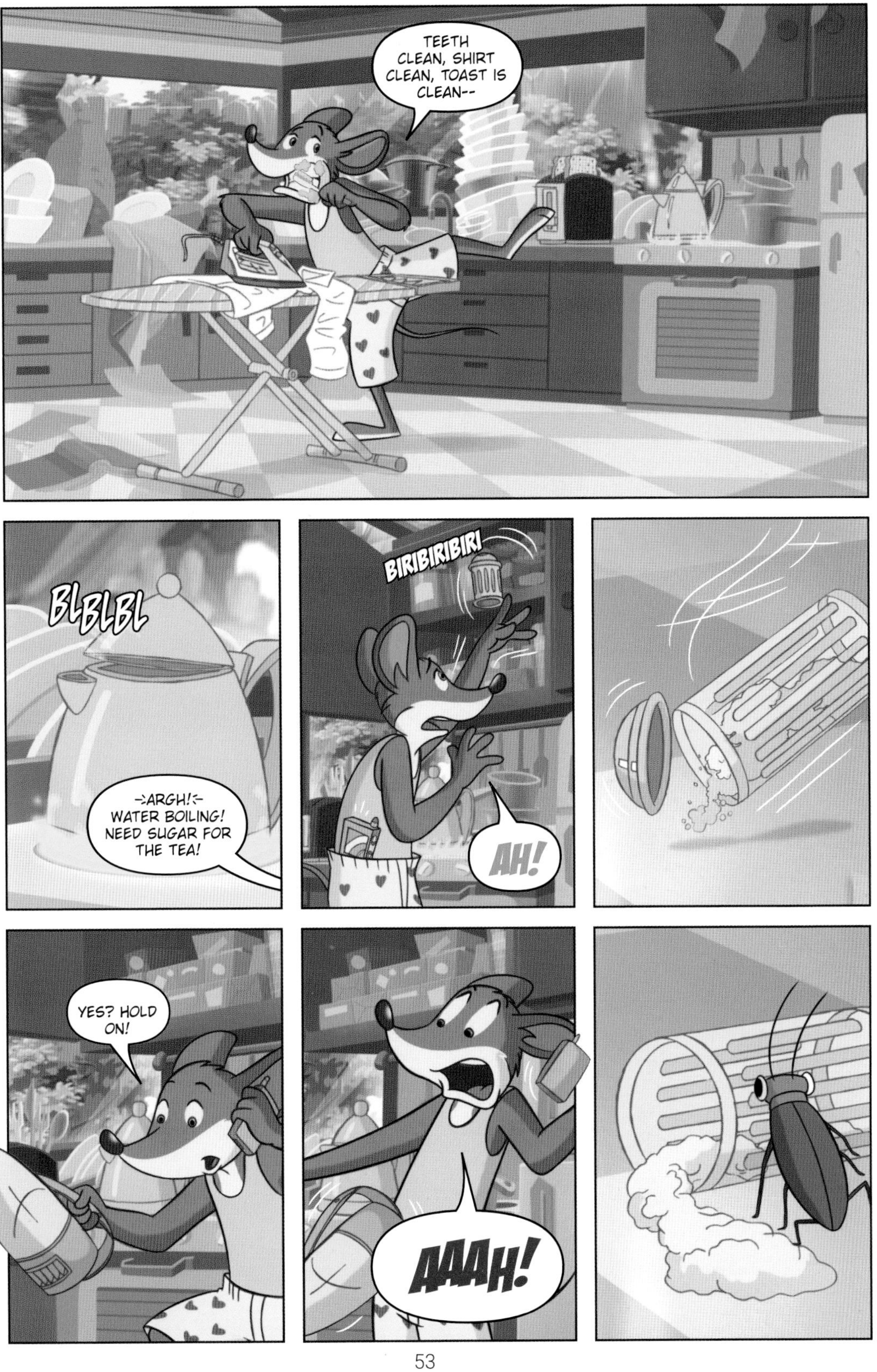
TEETH CLEAN, SHIRT CLEAN, TOAST IS CLEAN--
BLBLBL
-ARGH!- WATER BOILING! NEED SUGAR FOR THE TEA!
BIRIBIRIBIRI
AH!
YES? HOLD ON!
AAAH!

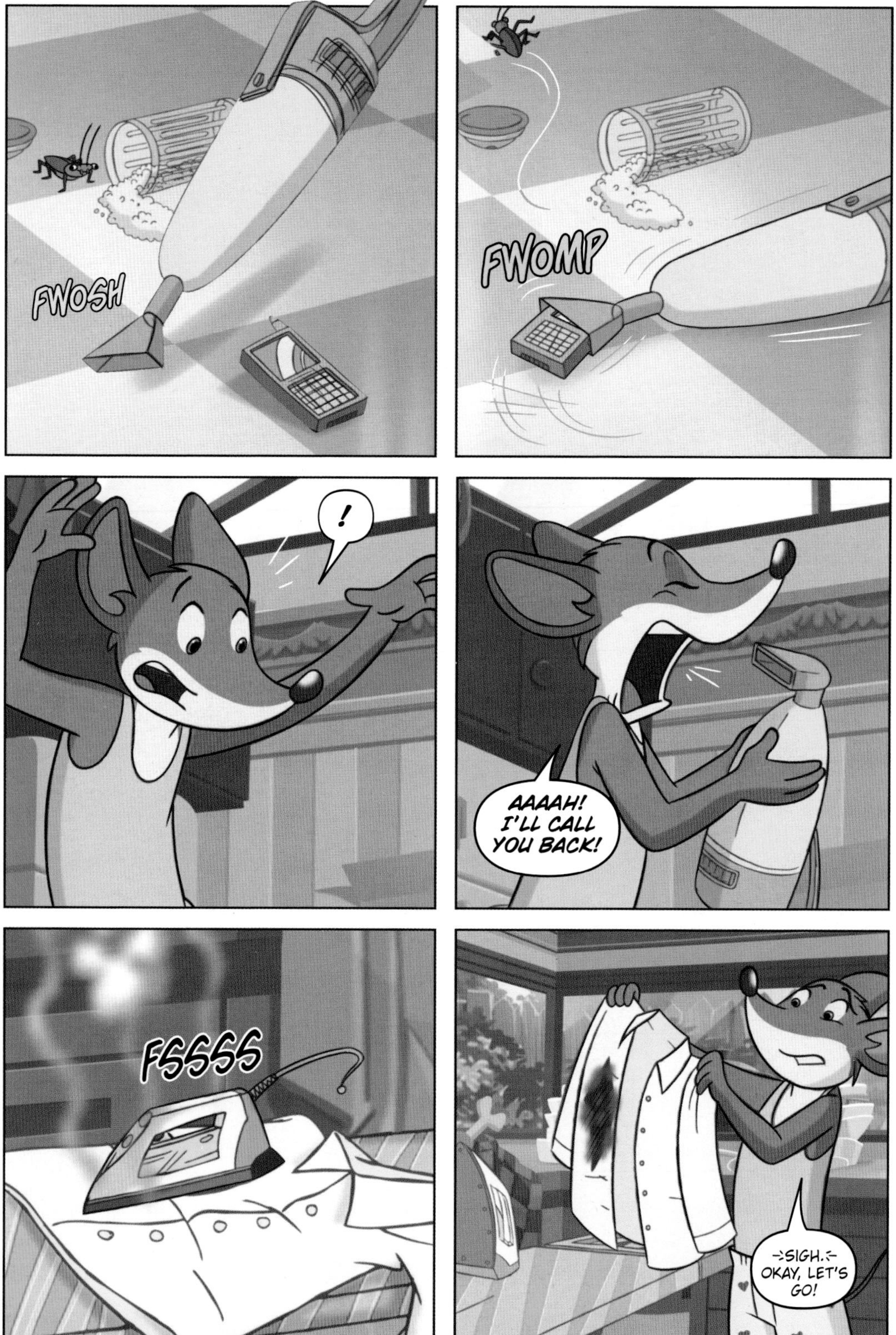

FWOSH
FWOMP
!
AAAAH! I'LL CALL YOU BACK!
FSSSS
-SIGH.- OKAY, LET'S GO!

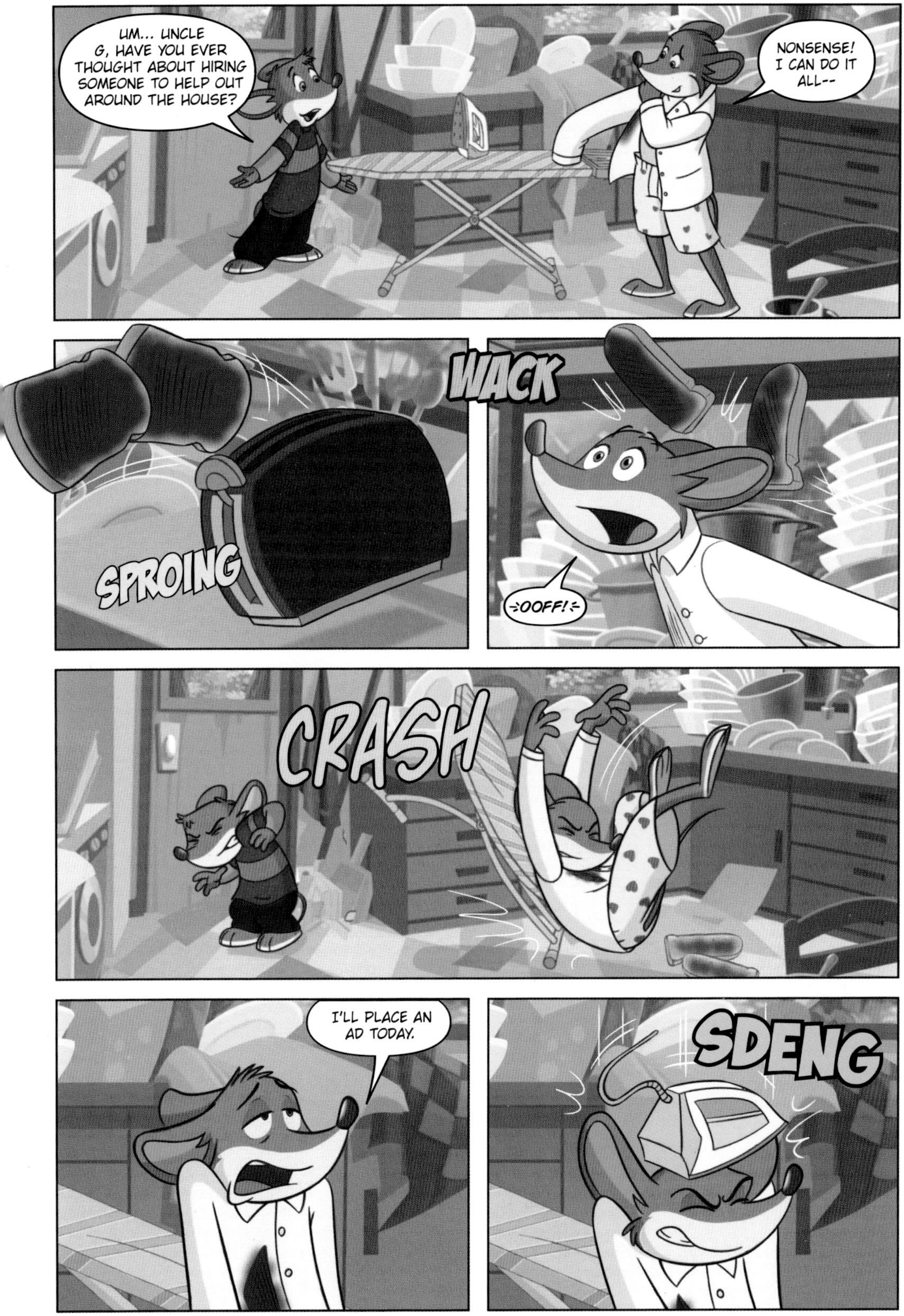
UM... UNCLE G, HAVE YOU EVER THOUGHT ABOUT HIRING SOMEONE TO HELP OUT AROUND THE HOUSE?
NONSENSE! I CAN DO IT ALL--
SPROING
WACK
OOFF!
CRASH
I'LL PLACE AN AD TODAY.
SDENG

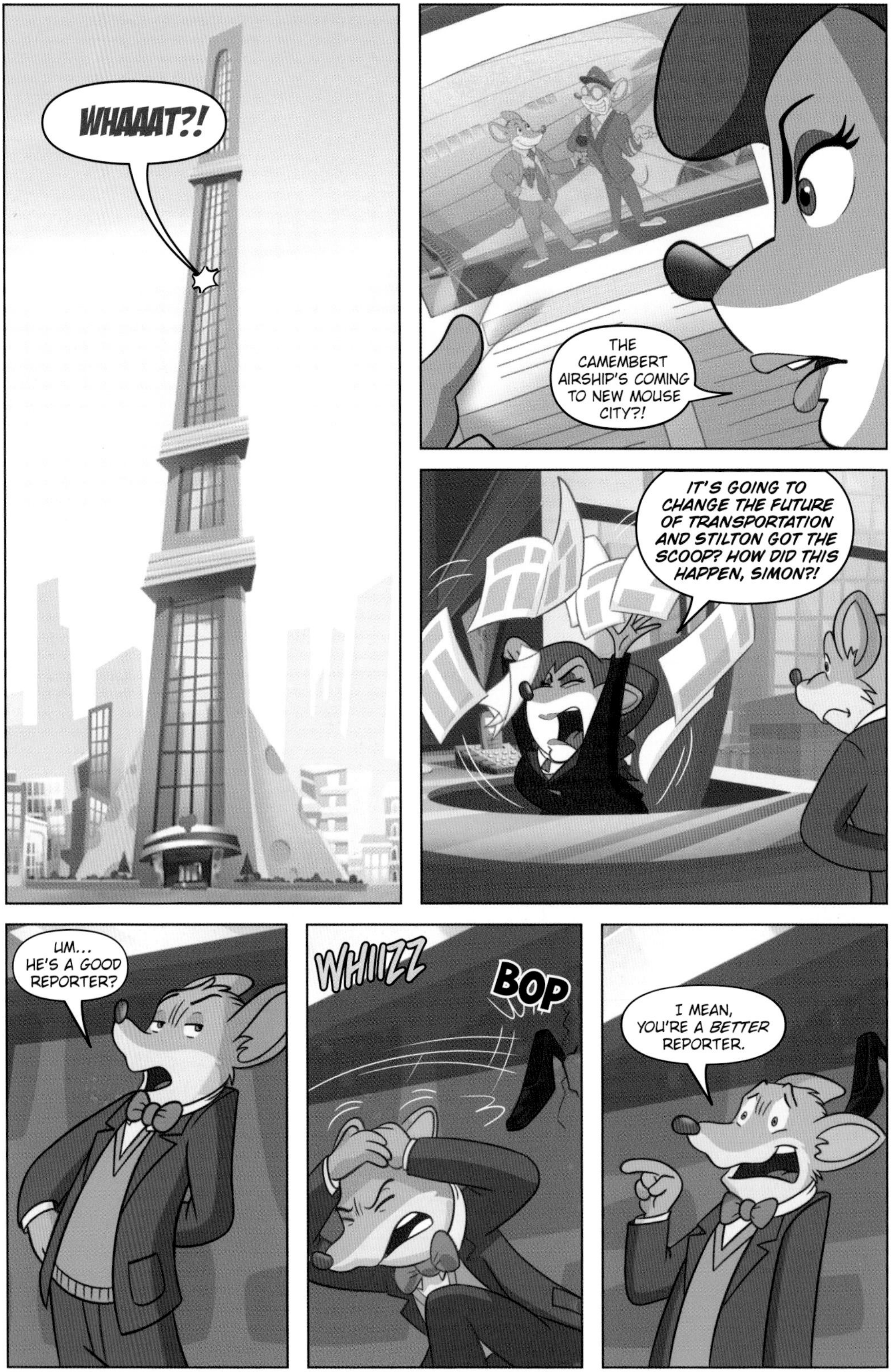
WHAAAT?!
THE CAMEMBERT AIRSHIP'S COMING TO NEW MOUSE CITY?!
IT'S GOING TO CHANGE THE FUTURE OF TRANSPORTATION AND STILTON GOT THE SCOOP? HOW DID THIS HAPPEN, SIMON?!
UM... HE'S A GOOD REPORTER?
WHIIZZ
BOP
I MEAN, YOU'RE A BETTER REPORTER.

Don't Miss GERONIMO STILTON REPORTER #12
"The Mouse House of the Future"! Coming soon!

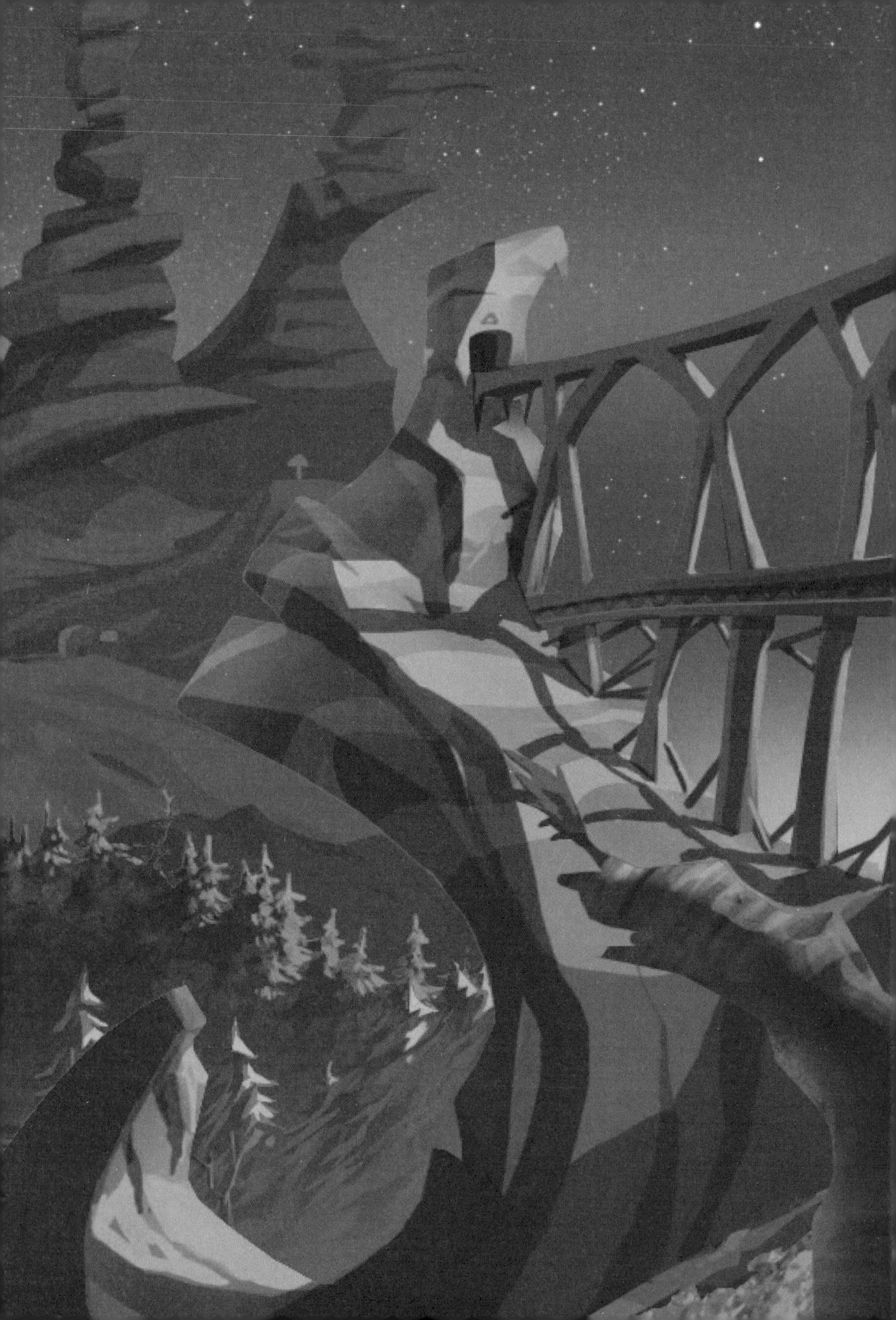